Shadows in
the Water

A

STARBUCK

FAMILY

ADVENTURE

Shadows in the Water

KATHRYN LASKY

Harcourt Brace & Company

San Diego   New York   London

Requests for permission to make copies of any part of the work
should be mailed to: Permissions Department,
Harcourt Brace & Company, 6277 Sea Harbor Drive,
Orlando, Florida 32887-6777.

This book is a novel. The author has created names, characters,
places, and events out of her own imagination. Where the book
refers to real people, they are included to make the story more
believable. Any other similarity between characters in the book
and real persons, living or dead, is coincidental.

Library of Congress Cataloging-in-Publication Data
Lasky, Kathryn.
Shadows in the water: a Starbuck family adventure/Kathryn
Lasky. — 1st ed.
p.   cm.
Summary: The two sets of Starbuck twins use their
telepathic powers and the aid of some endangered dolphins to
help their father catch a gang dumping toxic waste in the
Florida Keys.
ISBN 0-15-273533-X. — ISBN 0-15-273534-8 (pbk.)
[1. Extrasensory perception — Fiction.   2. Twins — Fiction.
3. Hazardous wastes — Environmental aspects — Fiction.
4. Dolphins — Fiction.   5. Florida — Fiction.]   I. Title.
PZ7.L3274Sh   1992
[Fic] — dc20   92-8139

Designed by Lydia D'moch
Printed in the United States of America

F   E   D   C   B   A
K   J   I   (pbk.)

For Max, a friend of the dolphins

1

So Long Adventure, Hello Boredom

LIBERTY STARBUCK lay in her bed. It was too early to go to sleep, but her parents thought that she and her brother and sisters should start getting in practice for school. How dumb!

You can say that again!

How dumb! You still awake, July?

Of course I am. Who can fall asleep at eight o'clock?

July Burton Starbuck, or J. B., or Jelly Bean as he was sometimes called, was Liberty's twin brother. His bedroom was in the turret that connected to her room through a small hallway of the old house.

All the twins in the Starbuck family—for there was a younger set as well—could communicate telepathically. Until recently they could teleflash their thoughts to one another only when they were in the same room, but since they returned from London, they found they could send their thoughts even when in separate rooms or, on occasion, when they weren't even under the same roof. The driveway experiment had proved that. July had stood at the end of the driveway while Liberty stayed in the house, and they had successfully tele-flashed their thoughts to each other.

Remote teleflashing, as they called it, had even worked fairly well with the little twins, Charly and Molly, their five-year-old sisters. But you could never tell with Charly and Molly. They were totally unpre-dictable and forever distractible. As far as July and Liberty were concerned, Charly and Molly hardly made for a good control group in an experiment.

Everything seemed to have changed for the Star-buck twins since London, where their father had been sent on a mission for the United States. But now they were back in Washington, D.C., in their comfortable old shingle house that stood in the shade of an ancient elm tree on Dakota Street.

Mom says we have to get back on a schedule. Our lives have been too disorderly since London.

Our lives were fun.

I know. Now it's so boring.

It's almost like—there was a mid-flash break as July resisted the thought—*it never even happened.*

Liberty and July paused and reflected on the in-credible months they had spent in London. There had been no school, no schedules. There had been adven-ture, danger, even fame! Their lives had changed, yet everything now seemed to be returning to a dismal state of normality.

What had it all added up to? How could life be so . . . so . . .

Boring! The word itself seemed to thud rather than sizzle and crackle like the rest of the thoughts racing through the telepathic channels that linked the twins in their turret bedrooms.

Had anything exciting ever really happened? Of course they knew it had, but were they any different because of it? They were back in Washington. Their Dad was out of work again. School started in another week.

In London they hadn't had to go to school because Zanny the Nanny, their old baby-sitter, had taught them. Zanny Duggan had gone along to take care of the children since their mother, Madeline Starbuck, could not leave her work to live in London. Madeline ran the biggest ballet tutu factory in the United States. She could not be absent from her company, Starbuck Recital Wear, for long periods of time, so every few weeks she had gone over to London to visit.

Zanny had convinced Madeline and Putnam Starbuck that it would be more worthwhile for her to teach the children than to send them to the American School in London. She had put together what she called the English curriculum, and the children had learned all about Great Britain—kings and queens, knights and lords, the empire on which the sun never set. Zanny was, after all, an elementary school teacher herself. But now even Zanny was going to have to go back to school next week, in Chevy Chase where she taught the fourth grade.

Zanny's not going to like going back to regular teaching.

Like? What do you mean? She's going to hate it! She's got another Kendall kid coming up this year.

The Kendalls were notoriously ill-behaved children in the Chevy Chase elementary school system. They were numerous and truly rotten: they were bullies, they beat up on other children, they drove teachers insane. Even mild-mannered, sweet teachers acquired crazed looks after two weeks with a Kendall child in the classroom.

There were footsteps now outside July's door. Madeline Starbuck peeked in.

"Are you teleflashing in there? I can feel it. You have to go to sleep."

"Yeah, but how can we go to sleep this early?"

"You children need to get back on a schedule." Putnam Starbuck, their father, had come to the door and poked in his bald head.

He needs to get a job, Liberty teleflashed, but of course their father had no idea what she said.

We won't have enough homework to keep him busy, July replied. *You know how it is at the beginning of school. They hardly give you anything. And he'll be asking us all the time about our homework, wanting to help us.*

Being a pain.

The children loved their father very much. But when Putnam Starbuck was between jobs, he tended to get overly involved as a parent. He became Super Dad, fixing healthy snacks for them when they came home from school, arranging family spelling bees so they could get 100 percent on the Friday spelling tests.

Mrs. Malthus, the housekeeper, fed them Popsicles and didn't give a hoot what the kids got on their spelling tests. Her goal was to present a clean house and children without injuries when the parents came home from work. But with Putnam out of work, Mrs. Malthus came to clean only two days a week, so the twins were stuck with Super Dad.

Madeline and Putnam Starbuck said good night once more to each of their children. This was their fourth round of good-nights to both sets of twins— that meant they had said good night sixteen times in the last forty-five minutes. They turned off the hall light and headed toward their own bedroom, which was just past Charly and Molly's.

"I think Charly and Molly are on the verge of conking," July heard his dad say.

Wrong! Charly and Molly were not on the verge of conking. Twenty minutes later Liberty heard the unmistakable pitter-patter of four little feet. The youngest twins were standing by her bed with their Davy Crockett coonskin caps, their noses running as usual. Molly was wearing her coonskin cap on her head, while Charly clutched hers and sucked on its furry tail.

"Oh yuck, Charly! Get that tail out of your

mouth!" Inch for inch, Liberty thought, these were two of the most disgusting little five-year-olds in the universe—snotty noses and wet fur. "So what's the problem this time?" Liberty sighed. She had more than a sneaking suspicion what it was.

"The ax murderer," Molly whimpered in a small voice. Her red hair stuck out in a frenzied halo around her head. There was a sickening smell of perspiration mingled with mousse. The little twins loved hair mousse.

"It's really scary!" Charly said in a whispery voice. She started to put the tail back in her mouth, but then remembered.

"The ax murderer." Liberty spat out the words. "I could just kill that little twerp Felicity Farnham for ever telling you that bunch of rot. She brings out the ax murderer in me!"

Liberty sat up in bed and turned on her night-light. The little twins blinked. Light did not improve their appearance. Their upper lips were glazed with snot. Of the twenty fingers on the hands of the youngest Starbuck twins, at least eight had press-on nails painted a color that, as Putnam said, was never to be found in nature.

"Mom's told you time and time again never to sleep in your press-on nails. You could poke your eyes out. That is a much greater danger for you guys than the ax murderer."

"But we saw it!" protested Molly.

"Saw what?" Liberty asked.

"The ax," Charly said.

"Almost . . . we got to ninety-eight and quit."

"Jeez Louise!" Liberty slapped her forehead and fell back against her pillows. She could kill Felicity Farnham.

Felicity had told Charly and Molly that if you went into a dark room, stood in front of a mirror, and said the words *Bloody Mary* one hundred times, an ax would slash through the darkness and chop off your head. The twins had been unable to go to sleep with the lights off for a week now.

The more Liberty thought about it, the more she realized that it was this disruption in the little twins' schedule that made their parents so hyper about schedules in general. Wasn't that always the way it was? Once one kid acts up all the other kids have to suffer. Of course in this case it had been two kids acting up, seeing as they were twins.

Although not every emotion was shared between the twins, there was one exception—fear. Generally if one twin experienced fear, the other twin felt it, too. So now, because Charly and Molly were in the grip of fear, fear of having their heads chopped off, they could not sleep. And because they could not sleep they had become cranky. And because Putnam Starbuck was out of work, he had to deal with their crankiness and could not manage it.

Mrs. Malthus, on the other hand, would have just

given them a Fudgsicle and told them to get lost. But Put had offered them granola and psychology, and then had come to the alarming conclusion that the whole family was out of whack and had to start getting to bed by eight o'clock to get ready for a normal school schedule—something they hadn't had in ages.

Parents were addicted to normality. They couldn't handle a little ax-murder scare at all. But Liberty was sick of the little twins' problems dictating her life. She decided right then and there to step in and take on the ax-murder issue. Maybe if their parents thought Charly and Molly were getting over this, they might let up on all the schedule stuff. But now the little twins were standing here trembling, armed with press-on nails, slimy with tears and snot.

"This is nonsense," Liberty began slowly. "There is nothing to be afraid of. You must know by now that Felicity Farnham is a complete jerk." She paused. "You don't believe me, Charly?"

Charly had put her hat on her head and looked out cautiously from under the fur.

"Felicity is incredibly stupid, Charly. She would have to be. Remember what she let you do?"

The little twins nodded slowly. Their cheeks flared red as they recalled the trouble they had gotten into when they convinced Felicity to let them give her dog, Chiclet, a hair permanent, or a fur one, in their traveling beauty shop, Bú-Tee-On-Wheels. There had been big trouble over that.

"You think it was smart to let you two do that?" Liberty persisted. "The poor dog nearly died."

"It didn't nearly die. It was just allergic," Molly said.

"It was fifty dollars at the vet's office," July said. He had entered through the connecting hallway when he heard the little twins. "The ax murderer again?" he asked, leaning against the door frame. His jet black hair fell in a thick slash across his forehead.

"How'd you guess?" Liberty replied. "You two have got to understand," she said, looking at Charly and Molly. "Felicity is just trying to get back at you. That's why she told you this ax thing."

There was a sound at the end of the hall. A door creaked. The little twins jumped.

"I'm hearing voices! Somebody up?"

"Nothing, Dad," Liberty called.

The twins switched to their telepathic channels.

They wouldn't be caught up with this ax thing if life weren't so boring, July teleflashed. *If they had something really exciting to think about . . .*

Right, replied Liberty. *That's our problem these days. Acute boredom.*

Not so cute!

Come on, Liberty flashed. *I'll take you two back to bed.*

Liberty led Charly and Molly tiptoeing down the hallway. She found two flashlights so that the little twins could sleep with them under their pillows and flash them on immediately at the first glint of an ax blade. She tucked the twins in, promising them candy in the morning if they stayed put. She even said if they were really good she might play Monopoly with them, which was more difficult than any of the seven tasks of Hercules, seeing as the twins' mathematical skills were shaky, they didn't read all that well, and they were inclined toward cheating in board games. On a frustration level, playing Monopoly with Charly and Molly was a solid ten.

Please go to sleep! Liberty flashed.

But July's right, nothing exciting ever happens anymore, Charly replied.

It's so boring, Molly flashed.

Well, life can't always be exciting. Oh dear, Liberty thought. She was beginning to sound like a grown-up. How dreadful. Well, maybe something unboring would happen. One could always hope.

Liberty walked out of the little twins' room and turned down the hall toward her own. It sounded as if July might be asleep. She crawled into bed. The branch of the elm outside her window almost brushed the panes, and the moonlit leaves printed a shadowy design on her curtains. It was more fun to think of them not as leaves but as something else: to read pictures and figures into them the way one could find animals in the clouds. Liberty thought the oval-shaped leaves swam across the moon-bleached curtains like schools of fish.

But there was the quick feeling of fall in the air. Those leaves would soon turn bright colors, and it would be time for plaid skirts and shoes with socks, new spiral notebooks and pencil boxes, and all the stuff that was supposed to make you feel great about going back to school—and about being on a schedule again. It was so long to bare feet and Popsicles anytime, to shorts and wet bathing suits. But of course they really hadn't had any of those, for they had been in London. So for the Starbuck children it was simply this: So long adventure, hello boredom.

2

Singing Fat Ladies

SOMETHING WAS TUGGING on Liberty's sheet. She turned over and buried her face deeper in the pillow.

Wake up! Wake up!

It was a double-whammy tele-alarm. Liberty rolled over. Her eyes were still gunky, so only one opened. But two little twins fit into that one eye's vision. Good grief, did they sleep in those coonskin caps?

Open the other eye, Liberty, Charly commanded.

Not the gosh-darned ax murderer again, puleeeze!

Worse! Molly flashed.

Worse? Liberty pulled her other eye open. *What are you flashing about?*

Remember Aunt Honey and the Think Thin Diet Center?

Yes. Liberty began to get a dreadful feeling in the pit of her stomach. She rose partway up in bed and propped herself on her elbow. *What time is it anyway?*

Morning. And Aunt Honey's already called.

What about? A feeling of absolute dread was washing

through Liberty. Aunt Honey always did this to her. Soon it would not just be a pang in her stomach, but an ache. Pepto Bismol time!

The Think Thin Diet Center. Dad's going into business with her. Charly and Molly both wore tiny smiles. It was not that they were happy about their father going into business with their Aunt Honey. The twins were smiling because they knew they had delivered Big News, and it was always July and Liberty to whom people listened. Their older brother and sister always had big important things to say. So even if this was not good news, it was Big News, and this time Charly and Molly had been the ones to deliver it.

He's what? Liberty's exclamation thundered through the channels. July was in the room in a flash. *What?*

Again smiles wreathed the little twins' faces.

Daddy's going into business with Aunt Honey.

The Think Thin Diet Center? July was aghast. He couldn't believe it. Their spiral into terminal boredom now seemed set forever. Their only hope had been that their father would get another wonderful job that took them to someplace exciting. The Think Thin Diet Center was half a mile from their house, and Aunt Honey would be over all the time. How could their father do this to them? How could he do it to himself? He couldn't bear Aunt Honey. He found her almost as impossible as the kids did. Why would he ever chain himself to her in business?

Are you absolutely sure?

We heard him on the phone with her this morning.

This morning? It's only seven-thirty now. Aunt Honey never gets up until nine-thirty at the earliest.

It was her, Molly flashed.

How come you're so sure? Liberty asked. *What did he say that made you think it was Aunt Honey?*

A look of great confidence swept across the little twins' faces. *He said,* Charly began, *"It's not over till the fat lady sings."*

Liberty and July looked at each other. They were almost sure that was an expression they had heard somewhere else.

Are you sure that's what he said?

Yes.

Did you hear him say anything like, "Well, Aunt Honey, I'm going into business with you?"

Well . . . er . . .

Uh . . . er . . .

Charly and Molly's telecommunication seemed to frazzle a bit.

I don't think it sounds like it's for sure. July's teleflash was tinged with hope.

Well, there's only one way to find out.

What's that? Molly asked.

Ask.

The twins, all four of them, clambered downstairs and into the kitchen. Although it was not a school morning, Madeline Starbuck had been up for an hour and was racing around in her jogging shoes making breakfast for Putnam. In another fifteen minutes she would slip out of her jogging shoes into her high heels and suit jacket, grab her briefcase with the sketches for the spring tutus and recital costumes, and head off for her factory in Chevy Chase forty minutes away.

"What are you all doing up so bright and early?" She smiled at her children. Before they had time to answer she turned to Put. "Look, just when we get them on the back-to-school schedule, it's all out the window!"

"What do you mean out the window?" Liberty and July almost barked the question in unison.

"A surprise, kids!" Putnam exclaimed, pushing his glasses onto the shiny dome of his bald head. Liberty's heart began to thud. Could it be? She dared not think.

Maybe.

Oh, I can't believe it.

Is it possible?

The telepathic channels swirled with half-dared wishes and shadows of dreams.

"We, my dear children, are going to the Keys."

"The keys?" all the twins echoed.

"The keys to what?" asked Molly.

"The Florida Keys—they're islands off the tip of Florida. They kind of dribble into the Gulf of Mexico on one side and the Atlantic on the other," Put said.

"What about the singing fat ladies?" Charly spoke in a small voice.

"What?" Putnam looked bewildered.

"Who?" Madeline said. She stopped in her tracks as she delivered a fried egg to Putnam.

"The singing fat ladies," Molly repeated.

"Molly and Charly said that you were going into business with Aunt Honey, starting up that new diet center with her," July offered.

"Me, with Aunt Honey!" Putnam was stunned beyond words. He began to sputter, "I was merely talking to Honey on the phone this morning, but I . . . er . . . yee good grief!"

Madeline finished the thought for him, smiling sweetly. "Children, my twin sister is not exactly, as we know, Dad's cup of tea."

Cup of poison is more like it, Liberty flashed.

"The last thing in the world he would ever do would be to go into business with Aunt Honey. How you two ever got that idea," she said, looking at the little twins, "I'll never know."

"Well, we heard Daddy on the phone this morning and he said, 'It's not over till the fat lady sings.' And we thought . . ."

Madeline and Putnam burst into laughter. Charly and Molly did not look amused, but Liberty and July started to giggle.

Go ahead, just go ahead, laugh at us.

Yeah, laugh at us. What are we supposed to think?

Yeah, they were talking about fat ladies, and Aunt Honey said she wanted to open that diet place.

"Girls," said Put, "that's just an expression. It

means, you know, the story is not over until it's over. If I recall correctly, it refers to an opera, a very long one, where at the end a large lady comes out and sings a final song."

"So what story is this that isn't over?" July asked.

"The story that I'm being asked to solve. I have just been hired by the EPA, the Environmental Protection Agency. A gang of toxic-waste dumpers has been dumping all sorts of disgusting, vile poisons off the coast of Florida. I'm to go down there and investigate and, at the same time, work up a set of stricter guidelines for the disposal of toxic waste."

"A dream come true for your dad," Madeline said.

"Poison?" Charly and Molly said at the same time.

But Liberty and July knew what their mom meant. Their father had worked for the government for years, first for the Central Intelligence Agency, then as an under ambassador to the Court of St. James in London. But he had always been a passionate environmentalist. In his book, working for the environment was better than being a diplomat to kings and queens or mucking about with all that secret stuff they did at the Central Intelligence Agency.

We're back in business, folks, our business, Liberty flashed.

You're right. July switched out of the telepathic channels. "So what about us?"

"What about you?" Putnam asked, with a grin as impish as a bald man with horn-rimmed glasses could muster. "What about you?" He drew the words out slowly. "Well, I suppose our first order of business would be for me to call Mr. Zoltrono at your school and send our regrets. Alas, the Starbuck children again shall not be attending school in the District of Columbia. We find ourselves forced to go to the Florida Keys, Pelican Key, to be exact."

"Pelican Key!" blurted Charly.

"Is that the name?" Molly asked, her voice brimming with excitement. The image of the singing fat ladies seemed to melt away.

Imagine living in a place called Pelican Key.

Imagine . . . Molly flashed back dreamily.

"Yes," continued Putnam, "we are forced to go to Pelican Key and live on a houseboat in Pirate's Cove."

"A houseboat!" all the children shrieked.

Oh, I think I'm going to die for joy.

Apoplexy, that's what I'm going to have.

Apo—what? flashed the little twins.

Fits, fits of joy.

Good-bye boredom, hello adventure!

"Helllllloooo!" A voice trilled through the screen door from the back porch.

"Honey!" Madeline said in a startled voice.

"I know, surprised to see me up this early, aren't you?" Aunt Honey did a little spin through the door. She had been an Ice Capades skater for many years, and although she had retired some time ago she always seemed to skate rather than walk into a room. "Well, for my new Think Thin Diet Center to be convincing, I think I should take off a few pounds myself, so I've been power walking early in the morning. But I'll tell you the real reason why I'm here. See this?" She held up a large shopping bag.

Something tells me this is not going to be good news, Liberty flashed.

Good grief, what is she taking out of that bag?

"Take off those silly Davy Crockett hats," Aunt Honey said to Charly and Molly, and before they could blink she pulled off their furry hats and clapped on stiff tan-colored ones with black visors and black braid across the front. "Attention!" she barked, then stomped her foot and gave a crisp little salute.

"What's all this about?" Putnam asked weakly.

"Well, Put, when Madeline told me yesterday that you were probably going to take that EPA job in the Florida Keys and you and the children would be off in less than a week, I just happened to remember my old skating partner Pink Stubbins. His uncle is the head of a wonderful military academy down there. So I quickly called and reserved four spaces for the children."

Put looked alarmed. "Surely, Honey, they don't take children as young as Molly and Charly. They're just kindergartners."

"Oh, of course they do! That's the beauty of this academy. They believe it's never too young to start disciplining a child. They even have a toddler program. I went downtown and got the uniforms. You know, Washington is a great town for finding uniforms instantly. I think I got all of your sizes right. So this is my little going-away present to you."

Honey began to unpack tan shirts with epaulettes, stiff skirts for the girls, and crisply creased pants for July.

"We can't wear our Davy Crockett caps?"

"Oh no, dear."

"What about our press-on nails?" Molly asked.

"Oh, never. Don't be silly. You're in the army now!" Aunt Honey sang and began marching, her blonde hair gleaming, her mouth flashing a grin, her eyes glinting behind the thick false eyelashes she always wore. Honey did not need a brass band. She was one.

We'll never be free! The children watched, mesmerized, as Aunt Honey marched around the kitchen.

"Discipline—that's what they need after all the excitement of London. You're right, Madeline. A child without a schedule has taken the first step toward juvenile delinquency."

"Did I actually say that?" Madeline was standing, dazed, with a mug of coffee.

"Well, you said they needed a schedule. And Ramrod Reef Military Academy is an excellent school."

"Ramrod Reef Military Academy," Put whispered in disbelief.

Only seconds before, the air had been crackling with the electricity of telepathic images of sun-drenched islands with exotic bird names and house-boats in coves of pirates. But now, like watercolors on glass, the pictures began to wash away before their very eyes. Again there was that sickening feeling they so often experienced when Aunt Honey came to visit, that feeling of overwhelming powerlessness. That feeling of falling, falling, falling into a bottomless pit—the Honey pit! They could not seem to reverse the fall.

Their parents were making muttering noises about decent schools being hard to find. The four Starbuck children felt themselves tumbling completely out of control.

3

Starbuck Recital Wear

STARBUCK RECITAL WEAR was located in a large cinder-block building in the southeast corner of an industrial park in Chevy Chase. A sign with a scattering of stars and the name Starbuck loomed out of a mound of freshly planted mums by the front entrance. These plants were changed seasonally. In the spring there were azaleas. In summer there were petunias. For Christmas there would be a Christmas tree. From mid-January until early March, regular shrubbery grew there.

The lobby was filled with gigantic backlit color photos of dancers, children from four years old through their teens, modeling the various tutus, leotards, and ballet dresses. The most dazzling and glittery costumes were always on display in the photographs. Of course there were several pictures of Charly and Molly, for although they didn't dance, when their noses were wiped and their hair was combed, they made an adorable duo.

In one set of pictures, Charly and Molly were the Yankee Doodle Twins, all dressed up in stars and glittery red-and-white stripes, with top hats and fifes. In another set, Charly and Molly wore the Cream Puff tutus, which were a gooey pink-and-yellow color and made out of twelve layers of tulle that stuck straight out. And there they were again in the Dairy Maid ensemble, blue-and-white checked satin skirts with frilly aprons and bonnets.

Liberty, July, Charly, and Molly had taken the bus and had arrived that morning about an hour after their mother. They knew swift and immediate action was needed in the wake of Aunt Honey's visit. This nonsense about a military academy had to be nipped in the bud. They had not gone to school in London, where there wasn't even the threat of attending a military academy, and they certainly wouldn't do it now. Their idea was no school—period! But they would have to act fast.

They cut through the lobby. The receptionist had told them Zanny was somewhere in the annex. Zanny often worked at Starbuck Recital Wear for extra money when she was not teaching school. Her mother, Rosemarie Duggan, was head of production and Madeline's right-hand person. As the children went through the double door leading into one of the cavernous production spaces, they caught sight of Rosemarie talking with some stitchers. She looked up and waved at the four Starbucks.

"Hi kids, she's that-a-way." Rosemarie pointed to the far end of the room.

The twins stopped. "How'd you know we were looking for her?"

Rosemarie smiled knowingly. She was a plain-faced woman with crinkly brown hair touched with gray. "Should I salute? Attention!" Rosemarie clicked her heels together.

"You know?"

"Yep, your Mom told me about Aunt Honey's visit. I figured you would be along shortly." She pointed with one of the three pairs of glasses she wore on ribbons. "I think she's in tulle doing inventory."

Rosemarie always had at least three pairs of glasses dangling around her neck, waiting for the next visual challenge. One pair was for close-up work, like reading or examining stitching; one pair was for distance; and one pair was for the computers. She had never adjusted to wearing trifocals. She claimed they made her nauseous.

Now she waved the children in Zanny's direction. She was secretly relieved that Aunt Honey had pulled this military stuff, for Zanny, her own daughter, had been dreading going back to her old teaching job. Perhaps this was the escape she needed.

The twins were now winding through what they called the tulle forest. This was where the untrimmed tutus hung. They had all been cut to the appropriate lengths, depending on size, and sewn onto the elastic waist-bands, but the finish work, the applying of sequins or decorative edging material, had not yet been done.

All the trim work was done in the annex, which was attached to the main building by a bridge. These untrimmed tutus now hung on huge spirals of wire that were motorized. A spiral reached up to a height of fifteen feet and had a diameter of ten feet. There were at least twelve spirals, and they could accommodate almost one thousand tutus at a time. The tutus were attached to the wires by clips, and the wires could be moved by pressing a button.

The spiral structures actually began on a lower level. After the tutus had been cut to the appropriate length on the floor below, the spirals moved up to the next level through holes cut in the ceiling. They would then travel on, by moving wires, across the bridge to the trim department to be decorated. It was an ingenious device. Madeline had designed it herself, and it had been copied by other garment manufacturers.

No one could help but be enchanted by walking through the tutu forest and gazing up into the frothy canopy of tulle in colors as dazzling as a thousand rainbows. There were all hues and shades—pinks and magentas, peachy oranges and pearly silvers, bright lime greens and canary yellows, aquamarines and tur-quoises. Some were plain, but others were printed with polka dots or confetti-like flecks or even rainbow stripes. There was no sign of Zanny, however.

"Maybe she's in a conference," Liberty said. They turned and went down a corridor off of which were several small offices and conference rooms.

The children caught a glimpse of their mother. She was listening intently to one of her marketing people. It was a concept meeting for the next season, they could tell. The recital wear industry worked a full year in advance. The samples had to be made up and ready to be photographed for the catalog by August.

Madeline was used to seeing the twins at the factory, so it didn't surprise her when they walked by. They often came out to help. She waved from the conference room and motioned them in.

"Hi kids! You know everybody, don't you? Oh, I bet you don't know Richard. He's new in marketing."

Richard said hello and looked a little confused, as people often did when they met all the Starbuck twins at once. It was rather like being afflicted with double vision. For even though July and Liberty were boy and girl, they looked very much alike. They both had identical bands of freckles across their noses, and their hair, although of different lengths, fell across their foreheads in slashing black bangs, which set off their pale gray eyes.

"Let's get a little input from our secondary target marketing group," Madeline said. She held up a sketch of a girl in a long, glittery gold wig with bangs and a jeweled headband. The girl wore a unitard, a one-piece leotard with the tights and leotard sewn together. She also wore a sparkly collar that fanned into a breastplate necklace, and a wide, sparkly belt to match. "What does this say to you?"

"Egyptian," July said.

"Cleopatra," Liberty said.

Madeline smiled.

"Toilet roll people," Molly and Charly both said at once.

The six other people in the meeting looked perplexed. "Toilet roll people?" the new man, Richard, whispered softly to himself as he looked at the strange little couple before him in their coonskin caps.

"Oh dear!" laughed Madeline. "It's the hair, isn't it kids?"

Charly and Molly nodded silently. Indeed the wig was the same gold tinsel the girls used for their toilet roll people—little figures with Styrofoam heads made from the cores of toilet-paper rolls. They had constructed an entire Toilet Roll Kingdom, complete with turreted castles and a bridge.

"Yes," Madeline continued, "we were able to pick up twenty gross of this stuff really cheap out of Taiwan. A carnival supply company ordered it but then went broke."

"Didn't you use it last year for the Halley's Comets?" Liberty asked.

"Yes, but we still have plenty left over, and guess what major traveling exhibit is going around the country next year?"

"What?" July asked.

"Ramses—a whole deal on Egypt, the pharaohs, the queens, the art. It's going to ten cities. Teachers will be teaching Egypt like crazy. This is terrific timing."

"So what about the plaid?" asked Mel, a plump man who chewed on a cigar but never lit it.

"Too expensive," Madeline said. "And it's limited. Somehow I can't see it having a very long catalog life. I mean, you do the Scottish lassies and that's it."

Madeline turned to Richard. "Richard, I have to tell you that to get thirty to forty bolts of a good tartan plaid is one of my fondest and most elusive dreams. I've always wanted to design a whole little Highland fling ensemble. The dance teachers of America would go crazy. But it's a hard fabric to find cheap. We just can't cost it out per unit so that it's profitable for us.

"But the medieval court ladies and jesters, Mel, that's great. And for the little Heidis, how's the feather inventory for the Tyrolean hats?" The children filed out of the meeting as their mother grilled Mel on fabric and accessory availability.

They went up the stairs and over the bridge. Above them, like slow-moving clouds, a line of pink and white tutus traveled toward the trim department in the annex. Below them they could see the huge tables where patterns were cut.

Women with electric cutters suspended from wires on moveable tracks walked around the edges of the tables as they cut. The cutters looked more like small jigsaws than scissors, and they could cut through one hundred forty layers of stretch fabric at one time. Beyond the pattern tables was the tagging, bagging, and bundling department, where the "cuts," or various pieces that make up one design, were tied into bundles and tagged for the stitchers.

"*Hola!*" Cory, or Corazón de Santis, the head stitcher, looked up from her machine and waved at the children. "*Cómo están ustedes? Niños.*"

"*Bien! Bien!*" Charly and Molly called back. Cory and a few other stitchers and pattern makers were from Central America.

As the twins entered the annex the air seemed strung with endless miles of glittery rickrack, strings of sequins, beads, and ribbons. They spotted Zanny between two immense spools of gold and silver lace edgings. She had a clipboard in hand and was peering at it intently.

"Zanny!" cried the little twins. She looked up to see four troubled faces.

"We're being put in the army," Molly squealed.

"What?"

"And we don't even get to carry real guns," Charly blurted.

"What in the world are you talking about?" Zanny looked to Liberty and July for an explanation.

"Zanny, remember the Kendall children awaiting you next week?"

"How could I forget?"

Zanny wondered if it was possible for spirits to sink and rise at the same time, within the same second, for that was precisely what she was feeling. Yes, she remembered the Kendall children, and each time she did her heart sank. Yet here now were her favorite children, and the last time they reminded her about the Kendall children had been right before they convinced her to go to London to take care of them. There had been adventure, danger, fame . . . and love! Could it be happening again? Life had been so boring recently. Zanny wondered if it was possible that they were all on the brink of a new adventure, and . . .

"I can't hear you with all this machinery going. Follow me."

They went into a small room that Zanny used as her office when she came to help out at Starbuck Recital Wear. There sat the bright green canvas bag with the red apple printed on it that Zanny used to carry all her stuff.

July spotted a fresh classroom record book sticking out of the bag. He had peeked over enough teachers' shoulders in his school years to have permanently etched on his brain the thin blue lines of the grid that made up the boxes for the dreadful letter grades A, B, C, D, and F. And that was the way it was. You were reduced to a letter in school.

You bet! And can you imagine what it'll be like at a military school? Liberty had broken into July's thoughts when she saw his eyes riveted on the new grade book.

We gotta do some fast talking here, July flashed back.

"So what's the story, kids?" Zanny paused. She saw where they were looking. "Oh yeah, my new grade book. Hmmph!" She expelled a small blast of air through her nose in contempt. "Not a welcome sight to many children's eyes."

"Zanny, we're on a terrible brink," July began. Did that sound too dramatic?

No way, José. Go for it, July.

You know, you could help out, too, Liberty.

Okay. "Look Zanny, what we're trying to say here is . . . well, the good news is that Dad's got a new job, in the Florida Keys, no less."

"Oh, that sounds terrific. So?"

"The bad news is that Aunt Honey . . ."

Zanny's nose crinkled in distaste. "Don't tell me. She wants to go along as your baby-sitter."

"Worse," said July.

"Worse?" Zanny looked surprised. What could be worse for these children than the mere thought of being baby-sat by their overblown, overpowering, interfering Aunt Honey?

"She's enrolled all of us in military school."

"What?" Zanny screamed. Horror slid across her face. She looked into the eyes of these children who were so dear to her—so intelligent, so individual despite their physical identicalness. They were, in fact, the most special kids she had ever encountered. And they would be absolutely the worst candidates for military school imaginable.

"Yeah, and they don't even let you wear press-on nails, can you believe that!" Charly smacked her forehead with the heel of her hand.

"Yeah, it's a free country, isn't it?" Molly roared.

"So, I think we need," Liberty spoke very quietly, "someone who really knows how to take care of kids and who is also a teacher."

"Yeah," said July. "It's been so long since we've been in regular school. I don't think we'd do very well." He paused and looked at the grade book. "I mean, I don't think A or B or C could really describe what we learned in London with your English curriculum."

"Yeah, I think maybe a Florida Keys curriculum would really . . ." Liberty's voice dwindled off.

Zanny looked down at the corner of the brand-new grade book sticking out of her canvas tote bag. Oh dear, she thought, all those dumb little letters to fit into the squares, and how could a D ever truly describe Ralphie Kendall? He'd been held back again, and if she could save the Starbucks from military school. . . . Gosh, the Florida Keys did sound good!

She stood up from the desk, reached into the canvas bag with the apple printed on it, and plucked out the record book. She held it aloft. "A is for Adventure." Her voice was whispery with excitement. "B is for Boom times are here again, C is for Can't wait, D is for Delighted, and F is for Fabulous!"

"Hooray!" the children shouted as Zanny sent the record book flying toward a huge scrap barrel just out-side the office.

That evening a harvest moon sailed immense and golden through the autumn night. A light breeze filled the thin white curtains of the window in Liberty's room. The shadows of the leaves on the billowing cloth leaped with the antic grace of beautiful fish swimming in a tossing sea.

4

Witches' Fingers and Crocodiles

"PINK!" JULY EXCLAIMED. "I have to live in a pink house?"

"Not just pink, dear." Madeline was trying to calm her son. "It's flamingo pink." She paused, then said, "Actually, from looking at this snapshot, I think it's very close to the pink I used in the Cotton Candy Darling tutu."

See, it could be worse, J. B. You could be living in a tutu.

The Starbucks and Zanny were standing on a pier while their father got final instructions on how to work the *Coconut*, the little outboard motorboat that would be theirs to get around in. Boats were the main form of transportation between Pelican Key and the rest of the world. There would be another boat, the *Little Coconut*, tied up to the houseboat.

"You can't miss it," the man said. "The houseboat is pink and the *Little Coconut* is bright blue with white trim."

July had been so fixated on the pink house that he hadn't heard the crucial part of the conversation. Put-nam Starbuck had just said that if the children passed their swim test and promised to wear their life pre-servers, they would be allowed to take the *Little Co-conut* out on their own, as long as they stayed within certain boundaries.

"What's the test, Daddy? What's the test?" Liberty was almost jumping up and down with excitement.

"Well, I think you should be able to swim five hundred yards—that's about a quarter of a mile—with-out stopping."

"Five hundred yards is not a quarter of a mile. It's more," July said somewhat vacantly. "It's one thousand five hundred feet. A quarter of a mile is one thousand three hundred and twenty feet. What's this about swimming it?"

"We get to go out in the boat all by ourselves!" Liberty exclaimed.

"Us, too? Us, too?" Charly and Molly were squeal-ing.

"With Liberty and July, if you can swim . . . what was the exact length, July?"

"One thousand three hundred and twenty feet."

"But you can't ever go out by yourselves, Molly and Charly, and you two," he nodded at July and Liberty, "must never go out alone. You must always go together. And, of course, never ever at night. And you must always wear your life jackets."

Liberty was listening hard, but it was as if she felt

somebody or something were watching her, and it was not the big old pelican perched on the post at the end of the pier who scanned the still water for fish.

Then, out of the corner of her eye, she caught sight of him. A little boy. At first she thought he was Charly's and Molly's age, but then she realized he was just small and was actually probably nine or ten. His face, however, looked old, old and hard and tight as a wet knot.

The boy was staring at all of them through eyes that were open just a slit. It was on purpose, Liberty could tell. He could open his eyes wider, but when she turned to look at him his eyelids slid down further, just like shades. Except these shades were for everything, not just for the sun.

His face seemed to grow harder, and it possessed an odd masklike quality. Then she noticed his hands. What in the world was he doing wearing white mittens? Were they mittens? No, they were bandages.

She tried not to stare, but it was hard, and from where she stood it looked as if his hands might be mere stumps under the bandages. A shiver went down Liberty's spine. The idea was creepy, but even creepier was the boy's face. Was there a person behind it? And behind the half-screened eyes, was anybody home? She turned away, but she still felt him watching.

"How's it going, Mabel?" she heard someone say to a large woman standing by the boy. "How's Robbie doing?" Liberty looked out of the corner of her eye.

She never would have imagined the woman called Mabel to be the boy's mother. She looked kind of old to be the mother of such a young kid.

"Oh, we'll make it. Long process, though. They got to keep his hands bandaged for a long, long time. We'll be coming into the clinic three times a week to have the bandages changed for quite a spell." She patted the boy's head and Liberty, sneaking another look, noticed that he seemed to scrunch up his shoulders and recoil under her touch. It was as if everything, every square inch of his skin, hurt.

Putnam had started to load the luggage. "Okay, Zanny, you can start by handing me some of those bags. I think we're ready to go now. Liberty and July, you grab some stuff, too."

The children, bundled into their life jackets, watched as their father started the engine.

He actually looks as if he knows what he's doing, Liberty flashed as the boat pulled away from the dock.

He does, July teleflashed. *It's not the first time Dad's been on a boat. Remember he used to tell us about all those summers he spent at some lake with a friend of his?*

I know, but it's just kind of . . . I don't know.

Weird, Molly chimed in telepathically.

Molly was right, Liberty thought. It was weird seeing their dad this way. He always wore a suit and tie, he had round glasses and a bald head, and the kind of work he had always done usually involved writing stuff down or reading. Now he was wearing a T-shirt, sunglasses, and a baseball cap, and he was actually driving a boat. This was a switch. Not only was he driving the boat with great ease and confidence, but he was looking at a chart and sounding quite knowledgeable.

"Keep your eyes open, kids, for the channel markers—buoys. We have to leave them to the left. The usual navigational rule is red right returning. This means that if a marker is red you leave it to the right when you are returning from the sea."

Where'd he learn all this stuff? Liberty telewondered.

I told you. He spent a lot of time on a lake when he was a kid.

A lake, July, not the ocean.

Technically you're wrong here. This isn't the ocean, this is a bay.

July was right. They were in a gulf, the Gulf of Mexico. The Keys were located off the tail end of Florida, in a southwesterly direction. On the east side of the Keys was the Atlantic Ocean, and to the west was the Gulf of Mexico. Some of the Keys were so narrow that a person could walk across them like crossing a street and swim in the ocean on one side and the Gulf on the other.

Pelican Key, where the Starbucks were to live, was not in the main chain of Keys. It was a mile and a half off a larger Key and was in a part of the Gulf of Mexico known as Florida Bay.

Putnam now swung the *Coconut* into a narrow

channel. The water was shallow, and on either side the mangrove trees were dense. It reminded Liberty and July of a maze. The mangrove trees, with their tangled roots arching above the water, seemed to creep out toward the boat, threatening to ensnare them.

"You can really get lost in these mangroves, they're so dense," Putnam was saying. "Kind of like blindman's buff."

"Don't say that, dear," Madeline said. "You're our intrepid guide."

"Don't worry. I have a chart. It's all marked. Once we get through this part, it opens up into a bigger bay, and we hang a left at the lighthouse."

"Lighthouse?" July said.

"Yep. Believe me, they need them here. These waters are thick with shipwrecks."

"Shipwrecks!" the children exclaimed.

"Yep, Spanish galleons, the works. Wrecking used to be a major way of life down here. Some people still do it, too."

"Wrecking what?" Liberty asked.

"Oh, they don't wreck anything themselves. People go out and salvage from the wrecks. It sometimes borders on piracy."

"It does!" Liberty and July blurted out.

"Well, most of that was a long time ago." Putnam slowed the boat as the channel turned a corner. "Now we have a new kind of pirate."

"We do?" Molly asked.

Liberty and July knew what their father was referring to—it was the reason he had been hired and sent here by the EPA. The new pirates were the toxic-waste bandits, outlaws who, for vast sums of money, would take the poisons of industrial America away and dump them, with no questions asked as to where or what they were polluting in the process.

"Goodness! The way is getting narrow," Put said.

Indeed the broad alleyways of water had tightened until the snaggly branches of the mangrove jungle reached across the water like witches' fingers to close off the sky above. The boat putted quietly under the tangled arch, and the blue sky overhead appeared like the tiniest pieces of a jigsaw puzzle.

"Watch out for crocodiles," Put said.

"Are you trying to scare these poor kids or what?" Madeline placed a protective arm around each of the little twins, who were sitting on either side of her on the boat seat.

"Don't worry. Crocodiles are very rare." Put chuckled softly. "There are said to be only a few left in this region and, of course, none at all when we get out from these mangrove channels." But now every stick and log looked like the slender snout of a crocodile.

There was a sudden flash of cobalt blue deep in the mangroves, then an explosion of white.

"It's a heron!" Zanny exclaimed. "I was just reading about them right here in my bird book. There are the most wonderful birds here, kids. We'll have to start learning all about them."

Sounds like the Florida Keys curriculum has begun, Liberty teleflashed.

Anything beats Ramrod Reef Military Academy, July replied.

For almost half an hour they followed the narrow alleyways and channels of the mysterious and secretive mangrove jungle. At one point the limbs of the arch grew so close to the water that everyone had to bend over in the *Coconut* so the witches' fingers wouldn't scratch their backs. But Liberty did not bend far enough, and a branch scraped the nape of her neck and snagged a piece of her hair.

"Ouch!" she cried.

The finger immediately broke its grip. Liberty didn't turn around, but she knew a strand of her black hair was behind her, entwined on a witch's finger, blowing lightly above the black mirror of the water. Tonight—who knew?—a crocodile might glide underneath that same limb, smell her hair, and . . . she broke off the thought.

And what? flashed July.

Forget it.

It was just getting interesting.

Never mind. I'll be glad when we get out of here. It's getting kind of creepy.

Finally the mangroves opened into a sparkling expanse of azure water. Frigate birds, looking like small, winged dinosaurs, seemed to hang in the sky without even the slightest flap of a wing as they silently rode the warm thermal drafts of air. Lush green islands popped out of the sea as if by magic, and the children wondered which one was theirs—which one was Pelican Key?

Click.

Did you hear that, July?

Click.

Yeah, there it goes again.
Do you think anyone else is hearing it?

Click . . . click . . . click.

I don't think so. It seems as if it's right in my head, way down deep inside. Liberty touched her forehead.

There were more clicks—they sounded like scattered raindrops before a downpour. But July and Liberty could tell that no one else was hearing them. The clicks were occurring within the telepathic channels, and so far Molly and Charly did not seem to be picking up on them.

"Look, they're leading us right into Pelican Key," Put said. "Our own escort service."

Liberty and July were now sitting on the floorboards of the boat. Their hands gripped the gunwales, and they rested their chins on them. In this position they were as close to the dolphins as they could be without sliding into the water and swimming with them.

"You two seem to be the next best attraction for these fellows after the bow waves."

It was true. One dolphin after the next would come alongside, roll over, and eye the twins with great curiosity. Their eyes, round and almost as big in diameter as a doughnut, fascinated July and Liberty. The skin around them was folded and creased in an almost human way.

Look, they have eyelids! They must be the only fish with eyelids.

But they're mammals, remember.

Well, the only sea creatures with eyelids.

Do you have the feeling it wants to talk with us?

I have the feeling it could be listening to us.

Do you think we dare reach out and pat it? Look! Look how it's turning up its belly as if it wants to be stroked.

Yeah, this one, too.

Very slowly Liberty extended her hand. The water rushed through her fingers as the boat kept moving and the dolphins kept apace with its speed. She reached a little deeper, trying to keep her hand from being dragged away by the streaming water. A tingly feeling went through her as her fingers finally touched the dolphin's skin. It was like nothing she had ever felt—like liquid silk running through her fingertips.

She stroked it very lightly. The dolphin closed its eyes in bliss. July began to stroke another one's belly. And then, just as the *Coconut* turned into the small bay of Pelican Key, the dolphins streaked off.

The jewel-blue waters were placid and utterly still except for the wake of the *Coconut*.

"Why'd they go?" asked Charly.

"Well, maybe they don't like civilization," Zanny said.

"They call this civilization?" Madeline Starbuck asked.

She was looking straight ahead at a pier, the town center of Pelican Key. There was one gas pump and a shack that leaned at an alarming angle toward the palm-fringed beach. The shack had a sign that said Grubby Duck Variety Store. There was a cartoon drawing of a disreputable-looking duck with a captain's cap eating a snow cone. An old man was fishing at the end of the pier, and on a piling perched a huge pelican. Stuck in between the palms on the beach were a few little cottages in faded ice-cream colors.

"Look, here comes the pelican!" Molly cried. It had lifted off the pier and was flying over to them.

"I guess it's fitting that this fellow should be the welcome committee," Put said.

"It's immense!" gasped Zanny.

"It looks like a pterodactyl!" July whispered.

The pelican hovered above the *Coconut*, its enormous wings casting a shadow that extended on either side far beyond the width of the boat. Putnam looked up nervously and pulled firmly on the bill of his cap. He cleared his throat. "Hmmm. Looks like this fellow is going to escort us in."

"Look!" said Liberty. She was squinting straight up at the bird and had a clear view of his head and the leathery beak with its wrinkled pouch for scooping up fish and straining out water. "He only has one eye!"

The other children looked up. Sure enough, one

eye gleamed brightly—a startling white ring with a dark center. The other eye, however, was just a small irregular dimple that seemed to pucker into a permanent squint.

"Okay," Putnam Starbuck was saying, "we are supposed to go around this point where the Grubby Duck is, and then we'll see a boarded-up house on stilts in the water. We go one-eighth of a mile past that, and there's a channel. That's our channel. It leads into Pirate's Cove."

The one-eyed pelican stayed with them the entire way, and just as they spotted the flamingo-pink houseboat tied to the pilings, it flew off and landed on the top deck of their new home.

"Wow!"

Neato!

"Ooooh!"

"Aaaaah!"

Oooh!

The air was laced with exclamations as Put cut the speed of the *Coconut* and they glided toward their home. Pink and draped from top deck to lower deck with tendrils of bright blue morning glories, it seemed more like some fabulous floating birthday cake than a houseboat. White flower boxes stuffed with primroses and petunias hung on every windowsill. Hammocks swung on the fore and aft decks as well as on the top deck, and a water slide pitched off the bow—the front of the boat—to deliver swimmers directly into the smoky blue waters of the lagoon.

"Look, there's another water slide coming out of that upper window!" July exclaimed.

"That's so you don't even have to get out of bed to get into the water. You just roll directly from your mattress into the drink!" Put laughed.

The *Little Coconut*, with a fresh coat of white paint and blue trim to match the morning glories, rode serenely on her mooring lines off the stern of the boat. On the other side of the houseboat was a pathway of pilings to which the boat was tied. Behind the path, a row of palms arched toward the boat, the tips of their fronds almost touching the roof.

"Ah!" sighed Madeline. "There's only one thing we can call this boat."

"Name the boat?" Charly asked in a puzzled voice.

"Of course."

Look, if she names tutus and colors for tutus, naming this boat is nothing, Liberty flashed.

Let's hope it's not something dumb like Mambo Mamas. Remember that one? July reminded them.

"I think . . ." Madeline was tapping her chin in a reflective gesture as they approached the houseboat. "I think . . . well, what else could it be than . . . the *Flagrant Flamingo!*"

6

There's a Lizard
In The Bathtub!

"FIRST THINGS FIRST," Putnam had said.

That meant the swimming tests. Putnam had measured off one quarter of a mile, from the bow of the *Flagrant Flamingo* to a piling down the pathway.

The children could only pass the test by swimming the entire distance. Liberty and July passed easily. Molly and Charly flunked. Before the halfway point they had to be hauled into the *Little Coconut*, grim and pouting.

"Don't worry," soothed Zanny. "You'll pass the test. We'll work on it every day. This will be our first and most important subject of the Florida Keys curriculum. We'll practice swimming more than phonics or numbers or anything else, I promise. I bet in two weeks you'll be able to do it, both of you." She wrapped them in one huge bath towel and rubbed them down.

While the little twins had been trying to pass their swimming test, Liberty and July and their mother had been unpacking. Madeline would have to fly back to Washington in a few days, and she wanted the family settled in and comfortable.

She planned to come down every other week for a long weekend and then take one week out of each month. This was much better than when the Starbucks had been in London. Madeline could only fly over once a month then. But Florida was a lot closer than London, so there would be less time apart for the family.

"Okay, you two want to share that top room?"

"Oh yes! Yes!"

"Please, please!"

July and Liberty were jumping up and down. They had never seen such a wonderful bedroom in their lives.

"It might be hot up that high on the second floor, or rather, deck," Madeline warned.

"Oh, we don't mind," they both cried.

"There's a skylight, Mom," July said. "That'll bring in a breeze."

The room had three other windows, but Liberty loved the skylight best. It was stained glass. She stood under it as she unpacked her stuff. The sun was pouring through, and colored disks of pastel light swam across her bare arms and legs. When she looked up, she felt a flat pink rose glide over her nose.

She had never seen such lovely glass. There were at least ten blues of the sky, nine oranges of the setting sun, and five pinks of the dawn. There was, however, one piece of glass, only one, that was a unique shade of the palest lavender.

One window had the water slide, morning glories crept in the other two windows, and a door led out to their own private deck-patio with a picket fence and hanging baskets of pink and white flowers. There were no beds, just hammocks with pillows, and no bureaus—just cubbyholes. There were two small tables made from empty wooden spools, the kind used to wind cable or wire.

"Very basic. I like it," July said.

"If you call a water slide and a stained-glass window basic, I guess you're right," Liberty replied.

"There's a lizard in the bathtub!" A cry came from below. It was either Charly or Molly.

"I'm taking the quick way down!" July had not changed out of his wet bathing suit yet, so he flung himself out the window and down the water slide. There was a great ker-splash in the cove as he landed. He swam around to a ladder at the end of the *Flagrant Flamingo*. Liberty went down the stairs and walked through the salon, which was what Put said you called a living room on a boat, to the bathroom, which on a boat was called a head.

Sure enough, there was a small chameleon frozen in fear in the middle of the pink tub.

"The color of this tub must really be a challenge to a chameleon," said Putnam. Indeed the pink porcelain of the tub was another color not to be found in nature, not even on a flamingo. It was hard to imagine

a chameleon trying to camouflage itself in this situation. The small lizard was turning a musky dusky color.

"Will it stay there forever?" Molly asked. She was
shivering in her wet bathing suit.

"No," said Zanny. "But you might be able to coax
it out or into a box and then set it free outside."

"Why can't it turn pink?" Charly wanted to know.

"Well, I think it is trying," Put said, peering at the
little lizard. "But I just don't think that this pink is in
its repertoire of colors."

"What's a 'repertwerp'?" Molly asked.

"You know, its range . . . its biological palette, so
to speak."

Oh, that really explains it, Dad! Liberty teleblurted.

*"Biological palette." Sometimes this guy does get carried
away!* July replied.

"What colors can he turn?" Charly asked.

"Oh, green like the palm fronds, or tan like tree
trunks, or dark brown like a wet log. You know, colors
in nature."

"We could do an experiment," Molly said between
her chattering teeth.

"What's that?" Zanny said eagerly.

Always ready to start up the curriculum! Liberty
flashed.

*Don't make fun, Liberty, this is a long shot better than
school, not to mention a military academy.*

"Well, in our Rainbow Press-on–Nails kit . . ."

"Ugh!"

"Ohhh!"

Liberty and July both groaned loudly.

"Shut up!" snapped Molly. "Anyhow, as I was saying, we got all kinds of colors—turquoise, purple, even gold. We could see if this little guy could match the nails."

"Neato!" cried Charly. "We could keep records and charts and write stuff down."

The little twins loved writing on charts. Madeline was always bringing them inventory forms and order sheets from the factory, and they played office constantly.

"Sounds like a wonderful idea," Zanny said, "but let's think about getting him out of the tub so you two can take a bath. Let's not frighten him, though. I'll go look for a jar or something."

"No problem." Charly bent down on her knees and reached over the side of the tub. She extended one little finger with a pale green press-on nail that had survived the swimming test. "Come here, little lizard," she cooed.

"Don't be ridiculous, darling." Madeline had poked her head into the bathroom.

"No, honey, that's not going to work," Put said, scratching his chin.

"You guys are so stupid! I don't believe it," July said.

"Okay, Pinky," Charly was whispering even more softly.

"Pinky?" Liberty said. "You're calling him Pinky?"

But then a hush fell over the entire family as they watched Pinky crawl onto Charly's finger and turn a pale green, identical to the color of her press-on nail. Charly looked up and smiled. "He'll learn how to turn pink in a few days," she said confidently.

"Here," said Molly, extending a turquoise fingernail. "Let's see how he does in the turquoise department."

Pinky did just fine. He turned a lovely shade of turquoise. And all the Starbucks, including Zanny, who was holding an empty mayonnaise jar, stood in the bathroom of the *Flagrant Flamingo* with their mouths hanging open in disbelief—except of course for Molly and Charly, who were cooing softly to their new friend.

The crescent moon, tinted a deep rose color by one fragment of the stained-glass window, looked like a slice of watermelon hanging in the sky. But if Liberty swung her hammock a bit, the crescent appeared in the orange part of the window like the smile on a jack-o'-lantern.

I like it in the blue part of the window, July teleflashed. *It reminds me of the lighter side of the dolphins—you know, where the darkness of their backs begins to fade into that blue-gray color.*

Do you think we'll ever see them again? Liberty asked. *See them?*

You know what I mean. Will they ever come again, come to us?

July knew exactly what Liberty meant. It was the same funny feeling they'd had in London, in the house in the mews, when they first began to feel in their minds glimmerings from somewhere else.

I don't know. I have this feeling, though. It's as if they're . . .

Waiting?

Yeah. Waiting for us somewhere.

But where?

I don't know.

Against a screen, three moths jittered in a frantic dance. A bird screeched. The crescent moon climbed higher in the skylight until it reached a clear, colorless pane of glass and shimmered—a bright silver arc in the sky.

July was soon asleep. He always dropped off more quickly than Liberty. She yawned now and pulled the light blanket over her. She was almost asleep. Outside a wind stirred, and the palm fronds brushed against the roof of the houseboat like a light rain.

She felt a wisp of hair blow across her cheek. A dark feeling swam through her as she remembered the strand of hair snatched by the witch's finger in the mangroves. Was it still there, waving in the night wind over the black mirror of the water, a crocodile gliding beneath it?

July groaned lightly. Liberty's fear came through

only as a dim pulse in the night rhythms of his sleep. Liberty looked straight up out the skylight at the silver arc of the moon sailing through the clouds. She concentrated on the arc and thought of those six dolphins leaping high out of the water like silver arches over the crystal blue gulf.

Deep in her brain somewhere Liberty heard a tiny *click*, and then finally she fell asleep. A minute later she was so sound asleep that she did not even hear the sudden drafts of wind, or see the great shadow blotting out the moonlight as the one-eyed pelican landed on the deck just outside their bedroom.

7

Turtle Talk

"WE FLUNKED IT, but we flunked it better."

Liberty felt something dripping on her shoulder. She opened her eyes. Charly and Molly stood beside her hammock, soaking wet, their red hair plastered to their heads, their eyes bleary with saltwater. On Molly's shoulder was a little scroll of seaweed. No, not weed, Liberty realized. It was Pinky the chameleon, dull green now.

"What are you talking about? Why are you waking me up this early and dripping on me?"

"Charly! Molly!" their mother called from downstairs. "Come down and get dry. Let Liberty and J. B. sleep."

"We wanted to tell them about our swimming test," Charly shouted at the top of her lungs.

"Sleep? Did somebody say sleep?" July groaned and rubbed his eyes.

"J. B.," Charly said, padding over in her wet feet

to his hammock and sprinkling Liberty on the way. "We almost made it to the halfway mark. Zanny says we'll probably be able to get halfway by this afternoon and maybe the whole way by the end of the week, and then we'll pass the swimming test."

"Great! You woke us up to tell us this?"

"Yep," Molly said. "And . . ."

"And what?" asked Liberty.

"Did you know there's a pelican on your porch out there?"

"You're kidding," Liberty and July both said at once and sat up so quickly they nearly tumbled out of their hammocks.

The door leading to the porch was split in half. The bottom half stayed shut while the shutters on the top half folded back. Through the screen, the children could see a pelican sitting serenely on the picket fence. It angled its head toward them and looked in through the door that was framed with morning glories. Slightly haughty, with its single eye trained on Liberty and July, the bird seemed to be saying, "The whole world's up, why not you?"

"I guess we should get up," Liberty said.

"Yeah, I guess we should."

"Zanny said she'll take us all exploring in the *Little Coconut* after breakfast, and she'll teach us how to snorkel."

The twins were out of their hammocks in a flash, and Charly and Molly went downstairs to dry off.

Liberty wandered over to the door leading out to the porch and leaned her elbow on the bottom half. The pelican stayed put. He didn't look so haughty close up, she thought. Or maybe it was because they were up now, and he approved. She could clearly see the dent where his other eye should have been. It looked almost as if the bird were squinting. There was a touch of the outlaw about this bird, Liberty thought.

I agree, J. B. chimed in telepathically. *Maybe he's the original pirate of Pirate's Cove.*

A bandit, that's what he looks like.

Right. Let's call him Bandit.

The pelican fixed them with his one good eye and almost seemed to nod.

"No, no," Putnam Starbuck was saying. "Poachers are only part of the problem, or at least those poachers of the two-legged variety. There are birds and raccoons and mongooses, and then there's the environmental pollution. You see, they eat these plastic bags because they think they're jellyfish—that's the main part of their diet—and they choke to death."

"Who?" Liberty asked.

They were eating breakfast on the aft deck under a pink-striped awning. All Madeline had to do was push the food out a little window from the kitchen, or the galley, as it was called on a boat.

"Turtles, leatherback turtles," Zanny said.

"Yep," said Putnam, snapping shut a report he had

been reading. "An endangered species, vanishing faster than one might believe."

"Is that one of the problems you're suppose to solve down here?" July asked.

"All the problems are related. The leatherbacks have not been put on the top of my priority list, but if we solve some of these other problems, we can't help but improve their lot as well."

"Why do they call them 'leatherbacks'?"

"Unlike other turtles, they don't have shells. Their backs are very smooth, with a hard leathery covering that is grooved. Perfect for swimming to great depths."

"Why are they endangered?"

"Well, for the reasons I was just saying. They make their nests on beaches, but it's not safe for them anymore. There are a lot of predators, both natural and human ones. The human ones are called poachers, and there are polluters, too. Also, lights get these turtles all mixed-up, and lots of the beaches where they used to lay their eggs have condos now. There was one place near a mini-mall where all the baby turtles, the hatchlings, got confused by the lights, and instead of running back into the sea they ran across the highway and got smushed."

"Oh, yuck!" all the children said at once.

"And jellyfish is the main part of their diet, but if you're a turtle, how do you tell a jellyfish from a plastic bag?" Putnam paused dramatically. "You don't. You choke."

"This should be your first priority, Dad!" July blurted out. "If this isn't, what is?"

"Criminal dumpers! It's getting to be as bad as drug smuggling. They're getting big money to take hazardous waste from cities and then to dump it. All sorts of poisons, like from hospitals and factories . . ."

"Not right here I hope," Madeline said, leaning out through the galley window.

"Not right here, no. They go offshore and into back channels. But that's just the point. It all comes home eventually. And then it's not just the turtles. Hypodermic needles wash up on beaches, and blood vials. A blueprint manufacturer dumps gallon drums of ammonium hydroxide someplace, people start choking—terrible, terrible stuff, ammonium hydroxide." Putnam waved his hand distastefully through the air. "I've got my work cut out for me here."

"What about dolphins?" Liberty asked suddenly.

"What about them?" Put looked over his reading glasses at his oldest daughter. There was an exceptionally grave look on her clear young face.

"Well, you said that a lot of the leatherback turtles die from eating plastic bags. Couldn't that happen to dolphins, too?"

"I've heard of dolphins swallowing balloons and dying," Put said. "But jellyfish are not part of a dolphin's diet, so they might not be so attracted to clear plastic bags, which could resemble a jellyfish. But none of this can help the dolphins, either."

"Oh," Liberty said quietly. She switched to the telepathic channels. *It's kind of yucky thinking about our dolphins gagging on plastic balloons.*

I know what you mean.

Our dolphins . . . I wonder why I said that.

July wondered, too. The dolphins weren't theirs at all, and he knew Liberty did not feel as if they were pets or anything like that. They were the wildest creatures the children had ever encountered, but they had felt some sort of link with them, or at least they thought they had. Maybe it was just their imagination. If J. B. and Liberty called them "ours" it was not out of a sense of possession, but one of connection. And it was positively awful thinking of these wild beautiful creatures gagging on stupid balloons.

I'll never go to another birthday party with balloons as long as I live!

Me neither!

8

To Sandy Key — A Place Better Than Barbie's

I AM SWIMMING through a jewelry box!

A three-dimensional magic carpet!

With their facemasks and snorkels, Liberty and July felt as if they had entered another world, a watery galaxy aglow with light and color. Sea plants and coral formations exploded like underwater firecrackers, and gem-like fish glimmered through the waving sea grass.

It had taken July and Liberty about five minutes each to get the hang of snorkeling. Charly and Molly were taking a bit longer. They were all in the shallow water just off the beach of the little island called Sandy Key, practicing with Zanny.

After extensive boat safety drills with their dad and Zanny, they had taken the *Little Coconut* out for the morning, packing their lunches, plenty of towels, sunscreen, and charts. Zanny had let Liberty run the boat on the trip out.

The *Little Coconut* had a small engine and a set of

oars in case of emergency. There was also a mast stowed away on the *Flagrant Flamingo* so the *Little Coconut* could be turned into a sailing boat—if their father bought a sail, which he said he would do. Zanny had promised to teach the children how to sail.

Within another ten minutes the little twins had mastered the art of snorkeling and had joined Liberty and July on the small reef.

This is beautiful, Molly teleflashed.

This is like where fairies might live.

Yeah, or even Barbie. This is as beautiful as the Barbie Beach Mansion!

Puleeze! Liberty telegasped.

You mean Ken and Barbie? You've got to be kidding! July telegroaned, as he floated over an immense knob of brain coral, with its surface of ridges and furrows that made it look like a human brain.

Yeah, you're right, agreed Molly, who had flashed it. *It really is much prettier than the Barbie Beach Mansion.*

Not to mention the Toilet Roll Kingdom! July added.

Liberty took a big breath, held it, and surface dived down to make a closer inspection of a sea fan, another kind of coral that waved in the gentle gulf currents. She watched as a butterfly fish swam by with stately grace.

Look here! July flashed. He had surface dived beside her and was pointing at a basket-shaped sponge.

Liberty went to the surface for more air, blew the water out of her snorkel, took another deep breath, and dove down again to the sponge where July had been pointing.

Shrimp, July flashed before rising to the surface for more air. Sure enough, tucked into the basket were several small shrimp, glistening, transparent, and speckled with red dots no bigger than pin points. They crept along the inside of the sponge. Liberty ran out of breath once more and surfaced.

"Hey, kids." Zanny had raised her head above the water and had taken the snorkel from her mouth. "You think you're ready to explore the shipwreck?"

"Oh yeah!"

"Yay!"

"Well, good. It's just on the other side of this island. We can swim to the beach and just walk across with our gear."

Fifteen minutes later the children were floating over the weed-draped, coral-encrusted remains of an old ship. The prow of the boat and part of the deck were wedged between great hunks of brain coral. There was some anchor chain left and part of a cannon. Hundreds of tropical fish, some with dots, some with bands and bars, wove and threaded their way in and out of the gun ports of the hull and through the mossy links of the chain. A jellyfish suspended itself like a pink parachute over the prow of the ship.

I wonder how old this ship is?

And where it came from?

Do you think it carried gold?

What happened?

Well, that's the easiest question so far. Obviously it got snagged on the coral.

July turned and headed back toward the stern and then continued swimming for several more yards. Soon he heard Zanny calling, "Come back J. B., you're too far." At that moment he was over some immense, nearly perfectly round rocks. They did not look as if they belonged with the coral. In fact, they didn't look as if they belonged or came from the sea at all, even though barnacles had started to grow on them. Zanny called again and he swam back.

They ate lunch on the beach—peanut butter and jelly sandwiches, Cranapple juice, potato chips, and Oreo cookies. The little twins jabbered away about darling Pinky, about snorkeling, and if it could count for the swimming test? No!

Zanny herself was busy turning into one monstrous freckle despite her seven layers of sunscreen. As her curly red hair dried in the blazing noon sun, it looked like another coral formation to Liberty, but for the most part Liberty and July were silent, their eyes steady on the water, watching where it changed from luminous blue to green to aqua—watching and waiting for the silver arcs.

9

An Encounter
at the Grubby Duck

THE DOLPHINS did not come the first week, nor the second, nor third. The weeks collected into months, and the children turned a deep coppery color. With their red hair, Charly and Molly looked like two bright pennies. They had passed their swimming tests, and when they were out of the water, Pinky went everywhere with them, perched on their tanned, bony little shoulders and running across their collar bones.

They had three more lizards in training—Ken, Barbie, and Madeline. The little twins often named their pets after their parents or their favorite dolls. They had big plans for Ken, Barbie, and Madeline—jewelry, living jewelry.

Pinky loved curling herself over the twins' ears. With her head hanging at earlobe level she made a stunning earring—or so the twins thought. But there was only one Pinky and three other earlobes to garnish; hence the living-jewelry training program. The rest of the family found the whole thing so revolting that they had banned Pinky as living jewelry from the dinner table.

During these months, Liberty and July had become proficient at handling the *Little Coconut*. They could sail her or use the motor, and they knew how to navigate through the shoal waters of the Keys and between the reefs.

Putnam was making progress, but not as much as he would have liked. He had been successful in convincing Florida legislators to pass laws with stiffer penalities for toxic-waste dumping. He had successfully introduced a public-relations campaign that made people aware of the threat to their own lives, as well as the lives of the plants and animals. Still, many of the worst toxic-waste criminals eluded Put and the law enforcement officers.

Zanny was pleased with all the twins' progress in the Florida Keys curriculum. From the children's point of view the curriculum was great—mostly swimming, snorkeling, and bird watching—light on math, spelling, and language arts. July had created his own special intensive studies program in shipwrecks and treasure hunting. Every time Madeline came down for a visit from Washington, D. C., she brought him books on the subject, and his dad regularly went to the libraries on the mainland and picked up books, too.

Kathryn Lasky

Liberty was not so interested in treasure hunting. As a matter of fact, she was slightly irritated with July's near obsession with Spanish galleons and chests of gold. Gold didn't interest her. Silver did. In particular, silver arcs that leapt from the sea. Would the dolphins ever return? Did July even care, or had he forgotten entirely?

What are you trying to ask me? J. B. flashed. They were walking down a sandy road from their houseboat to the Grubby Duck for snow cones. Zanny and Molly and Charly were ahead of them.

J. B. had felt Liberty trying to ask him something for days, but it was as if the question always broke up into static in the telepathic channels. This sometimes happened if the sender was unsure or fearful in some way about what he or she was saying. So finally J. B. just blurted it out within the channels. *What's bugging you? Something about gold, silver? I can't read it.*

Liberty had been on the brink of answering him straight out, but just then she caught sight of a flash of white behind a screen of palms—and it wasn't a snowy egret, either.

Fresh bandages, she flashed.

It's him. You see him?

Yeah, behind those palmettos.

It was the boy they had seen on the pier the first day. They did not know much about him except that he lived at the other end of Pelican Key. He went to

70

school on the mainland, but he seemed to miss a lot of days—maybe something to do with his hands—and so far they had not gotten up the nerve to ask Ally about him. Ally was the lady who ran the Grubby Duck. There was something about the boy that seemed to discourage questions.

Liberty had thought about this a lot—the little wet-knot face, the eyes held half shut, little slits that made his entire face seem like a mask. I can look out but you can't look in . . . no one home . . . that was the message he seemed to send out.

And then there were the hands like bandaged stumps. Were there any fingers? Liberty had the most dreadful feeling that his fingers had perhaps melted together and were nothing more than shiny gnarled lumps, for it must have been a fire that did this to him. She tried not to look at the bandages when they saw him, and she tried not to look at his face, because the half-closed eyes seemed to scream, "No admittance! No trespassing!"

That didn't leave much to look at, and it was beginning to irritate Liberty because she felt he was always watching them, and something had begun to niggle in the back of her brain, whispering, "No fair." She made up her mind.

What?

I'm going to ask Ally about that kid.

I don't know, Liberty, if I would or not.

Why not? He's the only other kid on Pelican Key.

He's weird.
So what? I want to know.

"Oh, little Robbie," Ally said, handing Liberty her cherry snow cone and then going back to fix J. B.'s. "Yes, he's a foster child—a 'special needs' child."

"What's so special about him?" Charly piped up.

"He's handicapped, dummy," Molly said. Her chin was stained dark grape from the snow cone that she had been slurping. Pinky was hanging from her earlobe and beginning to turn grape color. "His hands are capped," she added.

"Ohhhh!" groaned Zanny, Liberty, and J. B. at the same time.

"You're right, sweetie," Ally said, tucking back a strand of gray hair that had escaped from her bun. "He is handicapped, but it isn't because of those hands. His hands got burned playing with fire, I dare say—so let that be a lesson to you."

"We never play with matches." Molly nodded solemnly.

"Never," Charly repeated.

Could you throw up? Look at them, like little angels!
And calling him handicapped!
Shut up, you two, Charly fumed telepathically.
Yeah, you're the ones who thought he was creepy.
Hush, here he comes.
He can't hear us, stupid.

But Liberty wasn't so sure. Robbie had slid into the

Grubby Duck so silently, like a breeze coming through the screen door. They had not even heard its creaky hinges. He walked slowly toward the soda cooler, looking at them the entire time through his little slitty eyes, his chin tipped up slightly, which gave him a defiant, "Don't you dare!" look. But Liberty dared. She stared right back. She wanted to see how he would negotiate getting a cold drink from the cooler.

He shrugged as if to say that he knew exactly what she wanted to see. He flipped up the lid with his arms, Liberty was not sure how, and faster than she could follow he seemed to have dived halfway into the cooler. His feet left the ground. The top half of his body disappeared over the edge of the cooler. He swung back up with a bottle of orange soda pop between his teeth.

The children were mesmerized. Then he turned to them as if to say, "You ain't seen nothin' yet." He took the bottle between the two bandaged mitts to the opener on the side of the cooler, deftly flipped off the cap, turned to Ally, and seemed to flick his tongue. Something silver jetted across the space between where he stood and the counter.

"Got it!" Ally cried and, reaching up, plucked the quarter out of the air. Another followed right behind it.

Robbie walked slowly to the door, staring at Liberty the entire time through eyes that now seemed almost completely shut.

"Thanks, Robbie," Ally said.

The screen door slammed.

"Well, I never!" Zanny said. "Imagine . . ."

"How does he do that thing with the money—spitting it?" July asked incredulously.

"Right on target, too," said Liberty.

"I guess he really is special," said Charly.

"You think that's special, you should see him with a snow cone!" Ally exclaimed.

"What does he do with that?" asked Zanny.

"He takes his shoes right off and holds it between his feet—like he was some sort of chimpanzee—and he bends over and eats it. The kid's double-jointed, maybe triple-jointed."

"Well, that's special," Liberty said.

"Naw," Ally said, wiping her hands on her apron. "You kids don't want to be special like Robbie." Her eyebrows slammed together into a little knot, as if she were thinking hard about what it was like to be Robbie.

"What do you mean?" Molly asked.

"Oh, nothing really." She began wiping down the counter.

"What did you say he was—a frosting child?" Charly asked.

"Foster," Zanny and Ally both said at once.

"It means that something happened to his real parents so they can't take care of him, and he lives with other people. They call them foster parents," Zanny explained.

"He came from an orphanage up 'round Miami.

He's been bounced around quite a bit. He is not an easy child to handle, though he'd been doing okay with Mabel and Bert 'til this last incident."

"The fire?" Zanny said.

"Yep, and this is pretty hard on them. They aren't the youngest pair, but they could never have children of their own and have always taken in kids. He's the only one they got now. But it's a lot of trouble taking him over to the clinic every few days to get those bandages changed."

"What happened with the fire? Was it just matches?"

"Nobody knows, and he isn't telling. He never spoke much before, and now he's just clammed up." And then, as if to change the subject, Ally turned to a man who had just walked into the store. "My dad picked up another *barquero* last night," she said.

"He did, did he? I'll be," the man replied. "That sure is good of old Walt to go out there hunting for these fellows. That bird go with him to point the way?"

"I imagine so," Ally said with a chuckle. "He swears by that old one-eyed bird's vision. Says that pelican can pick out a *barquero* a mile away."

Every week people in a do-or-die frenzy to escape to America from politically repressed homelands journeyed in makeshift boats and rafts, even inner tubes, the ninety-mile distance from Cuba to Florida, or the longer stretch from Haiti across the Gulf of Mexico. Some people called them "*barqueros*." Putnam had told the children that two thousand had come in the last year alone. It was said that for every Cuban rescued, two or three perished in the Gulf waters. The Gulf had become a graveyard for the freedom seekers who did not make it across.

Valtero, or Walt, Sanchez himself had come as a refugee to America over forty years before. He sailed to the Keys with his wife and small daughter, Ally. Even though she was barely four years old at the time, Ally could still remember the endless journey in the little skiff, huddled under the tarp with her mother, clutching her rag doll as the fins of sharks slashed through the water in circles around their small boat. The Sanchez family, and the rag doll, too, had survived.

The doll now sat on a shelf behind the counter of the Grubby Duck and surveyed the scene calmly with her faded stitched eyes and mouth that curved into a gentle smile. Ally often took the doll down for Charly and Molly to look at. She would tell them how her mother, Rosa, had so carefully washed the doll's salt-drenched body when they had reached Florida, and restitched her eyes and mouth. Ever since Rosa died several years before, Ally had resisted redoing the mouth and the eyes, although they needed it, for she liked touching the stitches that her mother's nimble fingers had sewn.

The Sanchez family knew how precious freedom was. Walt often went out in his boat scouring the Gulf waters for the *barqueros*, the refugees in their makeshift boats. And the one-eyed pelican usually flew with him. Walt had saved many near-dying people whose fresh water had run out, whose boats were disintegrating beneath them as hammerhead sharks circled.

July and Liberty wandered out of the store and walked to the end of the pier where Walt sat jigging for yellow jacks.

"What kind of lure you using today?" J. B. asked.

"Slimy Limey and Purple Streakers early on," Walt replied. The words came out a little bit mushy, and with a Spanish accent. Walt had only a handful of teeth left, and the words seemed to cram through the gaps between the remaining ones and get tangled up with his tongue somehow. But July had learned how to decode the mushy hisses and slurpy syllables.

"You ever been over that wreck off Sandy Key?" July asked.

"Yep."

"Think there's any chance that boat was carrying treasure?"

Walt's shoulders hunched up and shook, his shoulder blades shimmied around under the thin cotton of his ragged shirt, and the sounds from his mouth were like eruptions from an active volcano. He was laughing! He seemed to find this immensely funny.

Good! thought Liberty.

What's so good about it? What's so funny, for that matter?

"Gold! Sure! Plenty of . . ."

Wait . . . shussh! July was commanding Liberty. Walt had stopped laughing and July wanted to hear what the old man would say.

"Gold all over . . . up there on Lonely Key." He had begun cackling again.

See J. B., he's just teasing you, pulling your leg!

How do you know, Miss Smarty?

Ohhh! Liberty sighed. She was weary of all this treasure talk and obsession. Boys could be so boring.

10

A Dark and Silvery Night

JULY STARBUCK opened his eyes wide. His breath locked in his throat. Was it possible? Those round stones, could they be? They had to be! The round stones he had seen when snorkeling just beyond the wreck had to be the ballast stones of the boat . . . of course! July had stayed up late reading. The rest of the family was sound asleep, including Liberty, who swung now in her hammock, oblivious to J. B.'s mounting excitement.

Every ship from those days carried ballast in its hold. The ballast was often rocks. This increased the ship's stability. Now July was reading in a book about Spanish shipwrecks off the coast of Florida that the treasure was also carried in the same hold, for it could serve as ballast, too. "Follow the ballast stones," he whispered aloud as he read, "and find the treasure."

J. B. got out the chart his father had bought them showing the positions of the Keys scattered through the Gulf. "Unbelievable!" he muttered. Lonely Key trailed right off Sandy Key in precisely the same direction as those ballast stones. Walt was right. The treasure had to be there! They would have to go— but, no . . . it was an insane idea.

He crawled into his hammock and pulled the light cover nearly over his head, as if he were trying to cover up the thought, banish it. No, absolutely not, never, no, he told himself again and again. Oh, would his dad be mad! He pulled the cover higher but peeped out one little opening.

The moon was full, the water dead calm. Not a breath of wind . . . a perfect night. Beyond the doorway to the patio deck off their bedroom, Bandit sat on the picket fence and turned toward July with his one eye gleaming. "Go to sleep," the one-eyed bird seemed to say. The gleaming eye had a hypnotic effect on July. He did not yawn but felt himself grow drowsy.

And then there were flashes, gold ballast balls tumbling through his dreams. But they had no weight. They bounced high like rubber balls and then began to float like balloons. Still shimmering, the balloons turned silvery and transparent like bubbles, and then began to burst one at a time, and each time one burst there was not a pop but a small gasp, like the short shallow breath of a struggling infant. And in his dreams, July began to have a smothery feeling, too. He pushed the covers back and the hammock swung wildly for a moment.

Meanwhile, Liberty, asleep and unaware of July's distress, was also caught in a crossfire of dreams shot through with silver. But there were no gasps or distress signals. The wonderful dolphins that had swum up to the side of the *Coconut* on their first day were now riding the crests of her dream waves, streaking through the veils of her sleep like silver ribbons.

The clicks swirled in her brain like the bubbles in the foam of the dolphins' wake. Where were they heading, these dolphins? Where were they taking her? It looked familiar, didn't it? And then one swam close up, right up to her own eye, and rolled over. The eye loomed so large and gentle, so round, curious, and full of intelligence. Would it speak? Then suddenly the eye shrank, becoming narrow, darkly opaque, reflecting nothing, like the slit eyes of a mask . . . Robbie!

Her eyes blinked open. In her dream she had seen the eye, the good wide round eye, but it had been so real. It was real! She could wait no longer. She must go find them. *A perfect night.* But what was that gasping sound?

It was July, sitting up in his hammock looking very pale, his chest heaving.

Right! A perfect night! he teleflashed.

Often the twins' dreams overlapped and fed off each other while they slept. It was, therefore, not so strange that July should wake up and agree that it was a perfect night.

But for what? Perhaps it was perfect for two entirely

different reasons. But both of their dreams had ended in clear signals of distress. What the source of the distress was, the nature of it, the children did not know. But they felt an urgency to go out in this night that was perfect for something. They were just not sure what the something was. They both looked out the door leading to the patio on the deck.

Bandit was still there. The bird turned toward them. This time the gleaming eye seemed almost to wink, seemed almost to say, "You're catching on!"

I think we should take out the Little Coconut.

Head toward Sandy Key.

Yes, of course, and then on to Lonely Key.

Where else?

July looked once more at Bandit. There were no orders to go to sleep this time.

It all seemed so right that the twins hardly had to discuss it. They pulled on their bathing suits, grabbed two waterproof bags, and put in flashlights, extra clothes, and towels, as well as the chart July had been studying. Their life jackets were in the *Little Coconut* already.

What are you doing? July flashed. Liberty was leaning out the slide window and ever so carefully and quietly pouring a glass of water down the slide.

Do you want to squeak when we go down? You know how skin sounds on a slide. We'll wake everyone.

She was right, of course. Leave it to Liberty to think of this. Moonlight struck the slide. First July went, then Liberty. A soft swoosh and they slipped quietly into the warm water of the cove without a splash. They held the waterproof pouches over their heads and swam a kind of frog stroke, propelling themselves with only their feet to the side of the *Little Coconut*.

Silently using one oar as a pole, July pushed them away from the houseboat. They would pole their way out of the cove into the main channel that led to the Gulf before they would turn on the engine. Liberty hoped a slight breeze would come up so they could hoist the little blue sail. It was so peaceful she did not want to fracture the night with the sound of the sputtering engine.

Before them, silver chips of moonlight were scattered on the water. Like a path, the chips led straight down the deepest part of the channel and into the open waters. It was so silent, so vast, and the two children felt small and insignificant. Yet they followed this silvery path that seemed to beckon them, draw them inexorably—to what, they were not sure. Each, now, was quite alone with her and his own thoughts.

July thought of ballast stones and gold and Walt's words. He hardly needed to look at the chart. Liberty thought of the dolphins, the great gentle and curious eyes, the wonderful silky touch of their skin.

A breeze came up.

Do you think there's enough to raise the sail?

Try it.

Liberty put the boom into the mast fitting and then began hauling on the halyard, which raised the sail. As if summoned by magic, more wind filled the moonlit triangle, which swelled into the starry night. The boat quickened as it was pulled forward by the billowing sail. Liberty made fast the lines, and July jammed the tiller stick into the rudder so he could steer under the power of the wind.

The wind just off the stern quarter, or corner, of the *Little Coconut* pulled them along the silver path under the starry dome of the tropical sky. The boat creaked and leaned a bit as if biting into the breeze. Around them, the sea sparkled with phosphorescence made by the tiny diatoms and microscopic aquatic plants that glowed in the night. There were the rustlings of the water against the hull, the foam of the streaming wake, the wind riffling the edges of the sail.

Liberty felt as if she were wrapped within a watery cocoon spun from the most elusive things in the universe—water sounds, wind, and glittering moonlight. Through the dark and silvery night they slid, pressed by the wind and pulled by the tide.

"There's Sandy Key just to starboard," July said aloud. "We'll follow the reef line another quarter mile to Lonely Key. That's the way the ballast stones trailed." And that's where the gold should be, thought July, but he did not say it aloud.

Gold, Liberty flashed. *I heard you anyway, Jelly Bean. You don't mind?*

No. She didn't mind the gold as long as there might be . . .

Silver! July chimed into her half-formed thought.

Yeah, the dolphins, that would be worth it for me.

For me, too, Liberty.

They approached the beach carefully under the momentum of the wind they had just quenched by lowering their sail. The chart did not show any coral heads, but one could never tell. They heard the gritty sound of sand beneath the boat.

Great! July flashed. They had silently agreed to keep all communication within the telepathic channels. They weren't sure why they had made this decision. The Key was uninhabited. Nobody would hear them. But maybe that was precisely the reason. Maybe they sensed they should be silent like all the quiet, wordless things of the island.

11

A Sigh From The Surf

LIBERTY AND JULY pulled the *Little Coconut* as far up onto the beach as they could. And then, as their father had taught them, they took out the anchor and buried its flukes in the sand. They sat down to catch their breaths from their labors.

Tide's almost high, I'd say, Liberty flashed. She had noticed the high-tide mark as they brought the anchor up. A thin line of seaweed marked it. Within another quarter of an hour it would be at its highest.

They wiggled their toes deep in the sand. The sand was much warmer a few inches down, for it kept the heat of the day and did not cool off quickly when the sun vanished over the horizon. Liberty looked up. *Oh my gosh*, she telesighed. July looked up, too.

The Southern Cross rose in the sky, immense, luminous, and so close it seemed you could reach out and touch it. Never in their lives had the children seen such a beautiful constellation. The light of the

Milky Way streamed through the sky like a transparent silk scarf against which the brilliant four stars of the Cross sparkled.

The children were concentrating so hard on the sky they did not notice what was happening all around them on the beach, but suddenly the sand seemed to boil.

Good grief! Liberty clapped her hand over her mouth. She had nearly darted out of the telepathic channels.

What is going on? July looked in amazement at the sand.

Are they crabs?

No, July telegasped. *Liberty! Turtles! Baby turtles!*

There seemed to be thousands of them, breaking through the beach in soft, sandy explosions. Liberty and July crawled on their knees to a spot a few feet away where the sand was flying in miniature gusts. From deep down in the sand they could see the little turtles fight their way out of the pits where they must have just hatched, their baby flippers working furiously.

In this nest, when the first few dozen or so had broken out and loosened the top sand, their little brothers and sisters began to pour out in great streams. Once out of the sand and into the air, their frantic activity seemed to increase as they scuttled for the water, which was just reaching the high-tide mark.

Look at them go! Liberty exclaimed. *This must be the gold Walt was talking about.*

You're right, flashed July.

"Oh, no!" Liberty yelped out loud. Like a scrimmage line, dozens of crabs had materialized and were pinching up the baby turtles. Suddenly the sky was split with shrill cries, and two birds swooped out of the night. July waved his arms at the birds as they dove down on the turtles. One bird got what it wanted, however. Liberty could see a flipper sticking out of its beak.

The twins burst into action and noise. In a tumultuous counterattack, they ran around the beach, shouting at the birds, kicking crabs with their bare feet, and finally picking up baby turtles and rushing them down to the water.

They worked furiously because within minutes the tide would turn. The water would begin to recede, and the journey would become longer from the nest where the babies had hatched to the water that they must reach to survive. With each quarter inch of the ebbing tide, the trip became more dangerous, the odds against survival rose. But Liberty and July would not let up.

There was no way of keeping track of the time. They had no idea whether it had been minutes or hours that they had been running around on the beach, but finally Liberty scooped up two wriggling three-inch babies, and July another three—the last of the hatchlings. They waded into the surf, ankle deep, and put their cupped hands into the water.

July felt something deep within him stir. He knew

right then that this life cupped within his palms was much more precious than gold. The turtle babies swam right out, stirring the phosphorescence with their little flippers. Of course, beyond the surf in the deeper water a shark might be waiting.

I can take on a bird or a crab, July flashed, *but I'm not taking on a shark.*

I wonder how many will make it?

I don't know, but at least they'll have a crack at the big time.

Yep, as Dad says, half of life is just showing up.

That was what Putnam Starbuck always said. It was a kind of adjunct to the family motto—*Sui Veritas Primo*, which was Putnam's Latin for Truth to Self First. Part two of the motto was *Apparere Es Eres*, literally, To Appear Is to Be, but with a Starbuckian twist it came out as, "Half of Life Is Just Showing Up."

However, what showed up next seemed larger than life. And when July had said "big time" he hardly could have anticipated just how big things could get.

The twins had just sat down on the beach, barely recovered from their chore of delivering the turtles to the sea, when they heard a deep sigh from the water.

Did you hear that?

Yes. What could it be?

I don't know. Fish don't sigh.

But it came from the water.

Oh gads, look! Liberty pointed to where the foam of the broken waves rejoined the surf. Heaving itself from the froth, spiked and ridged, immense and majestic, a creature older than time gasped and raised its head. Liberty reached for July's hand and held it tight. Phosphorescent waves broke over the huge dark back. There was another deep, weary sigh. *She must be seven feet long,* Liberty thought.

She's the size of a car—a Volkswagen, at least. They sat perfectly still as the mother turtle began her crawl up onto the beach. She propelled herself slowly, painfully, on her flippers, which spanned eight feet from the tip of one to the tip of the other. Her progress appeared torturous; her breathing, labored. The twins realized the turtle was here to lay her eggs, to dig a nest.

Look, down the beach! July pointed. Another turtle had broken through the surf.

The turtles proceeded slowly and silently, except for occasional deep sighs, as they made their way up to dry land. It would take them fifteen to thirty minutes to reach the spot where they would begin digging their nests. They seemed totally unaware of the children.

The twins remembered how their father had told them about lights confusing the turtles, so they were careful not to shine their flashlights anywhere near the turtles' heads. But Liberty and July watched as the first mother began digging her nest by flinging back sand with her flippers. She skewed her body about in the beach as if to make a comfortable pit.

She did this for several minutes, and then her body

settled deeper into the sand and her back flippers went to work. Slowly and rhythmically, alternating hind flippers, she scooped out large clumps of sand. Then she stopped. She seemed to be in an almost dazed state. The children crept closer, coming up behind her. She did not notice them. They came nearer still. She could not see them.

We could turn the flashlight on low, don't you think? Liberty flashed. *It shouldn't bother her.*

Not unless she has eyes in the back of her head.

They shined the light on her tail. Her flippers were spread across the nest.

Look, there's a big chunk out of her left flipper.

Must be a shark bite.

Or a propeller. Dad says a lot of these turtles get hit by boats.

But the flippers seem to work all right. Did you see how perfectly she scooped out the sand? I wish we could see the nest and the eggs.

We can, Liberty.

What do you mean?

Remember those pictures in that nature magazine Dad brought home? One showed a scientist holding back a flipper while someone counted the eggs.

Oh yeah! Want to try it?

Sure. Who does the holding?

I will, Liberty said.

Gently she reached for the flipper. It was heavy and very stiff.

Gads, this is harder than I thought. But the turtle was not resisting her. It was just that the flipper was a thick, heavy mass of muscle. She pulled more firmly to the side. They both gasped as they saw one, two, three shiny wet eggs slide out. They were at least twice as big as Ping-Pong balls, more like billiard balls. And they were dropping into a narrow shaft nearly three feet deep.

The turtle, oblivious to the children, was intent on one thing only—depositing her eggs. As she did this she continued to sigh and weep. Liberty and July turned off their flashlight and walked around to her head. They crouched and watched her. They could hear the soft noises of other turtles scattered down the beach, but they stayed beside this one. She wept immense, oily tears loaded with grains of sand. Deep sighs and ragged gasps tore from her throat, which had turned bright pink.

After an hour she was finished. Several dozen eggs had been deposited. She then began to flip sand back into the nest using her front flippers. Within minutes there was no sign that underneath the sand a clutch of turtle eggs was buried.

With another deep breath, she turned toward the sea. She moved more quickly now. It was a downhill run to the water. The twins followed quietly behind her on either side of the **V** her tail gouged in the sand.

They watched as she made her way across the shallow sheet of ebbing water that slicked the sand as a wave retreated. They could almost feel her growing urgency for deeper water as the thin sheet of surf slid back. They felt her relief as the first wave broke over her back. She was not yet buoyant, but she was so close, another heave or two . . .

Ahhh, both twins telesighed, for the turtle's relief seemed to sweep over them as well. Once immersed, the creature's fat flippers, clumsy on land, suddenly became wings, and the great turtle began to fly through water. They watched her as she kept her head reared high over the breaking wave, but then they lost sight of her as she took a dive just beyond the surf line.

The sky was beginning to grow lighter. Other turtles were making their way to the water. The twins knew they must get back to the houseboat or it would be big trouble, but they also knew they would come back. For how could they sleep another night in peace thinking about the little hatchlings, the baby turtles struggling to the sea? And how could they resist coming to this beach under the Southern Cross to witness in the silver silence a ritual older than time and more magical than fantasy?

12

The Great Egg-scape

THE NEXT NIGHT when the moon sailed high into the rose panes of the stained-glass skylight, the twins thought of the turtles, the immense mothers struggling up from the surf, the sand boiling with the babies, the crabs and birds waiting for them.

They'll die if we don't go, Liberty flashed.

But there are so many of them, July flashed back from his hammock. *We really have to get some help.*

According to that magazine, this is almost the end of the nesting and hatching season. It shouldn't be that much longer. The twins had found an article about the leatherbacks in a magazine of their father's.

But we can't go out every night. We'll get caught.

Let's just do it once more tonight. Then we can call that nature organization Dad was telling us about—the Keys Wildlife Guardians, or whatever he called it—and we can report it.

So once again the twins slipped down the slide into

the cove waters and climbed aboard the *Little Coconut*. They could not resist the urge to follow the silver path of moonlight to Lonely Key, where the beach would boil with hatchlings, and immense mothers, gasping and sighing, would heave themselves out of the sea to lay their eggs.

It was on this second trip that Liberty and July realized that the danger for the turtles began long before they hatched. One of the nests dug by a mother turtle the previous night had been too close to the tide line and was washed out, leaving the eggs exposed to surf and predators. So when they saw another turtle heading for a spot too close to the water, they quickly followed her.

We can re-bury these eggs! Liberty flashed. *Remember, we saw pictures of scientists doing it in the magazine article. They were moving the eggs to safer places.*

Just as they finished re-burying the clutch of eggs, another turtle crawled out of the surf and barely made it beyond the breaking waves before she began digging her nest. Then a third turtle.

Oh my gosh! July groaned.

Here we go again, Liberty flashed. *The Great Eggscape!*

The twins were excited and full of energy, but after hours of backbreaking work, they were exhausted. Just when they thought they had finished, and were resting for a few minutes before sailing back in the *Little Coconut*, another turtle came. They both groaned.

It's got to be close to daybreak. I didn't think they would come this late, Liberty flashed.

Late Louise, J. B. replied.

Or how about Mrs. Watkins! They telegiggled. Mrs. Watkins was the mother of their friend Henry and was always late when driving the car pool.

Where will we put her eggs if she lays them too low? Liberty telewondered. *We've used all the good spots high up.*

Maybe over there. July pointed. *I know it's higher up, but at least it's steep and the hatchlings can sled right down to the water.*

Let me scout it out, Liberty replied.

She walked to the place J. B. had pointed to. There was a small heap of seaweed, but she stopped when she saw what lay on top: a metal drum painted with a skull and crossbones. The word TOXIC was emblazoned on the side in peeling yellow letters. She crouched closer and read the smaller letters underneath: DI-PLOIDYMYSTEROL. Oh, great! Liberty thought. She turned to July, who was several yards down the beach, and teleblasted a terse message:

Come quick!

July, who had been watching Late Louise's progress from the water, looked up. *What?*

Just come!

He was there in half a minute.

This is not the spot for eggs. Look at this can. And who knows—the whole beach might be contaminated!

J. B. crouched down. He flicked a finger against the metal. A hollow sound rang out. *It's empty.* He could see it was rusted out in one corner. *I think it's done all its contaminating someplace else.*

But like Dad says—someplace else is everywhere with this kind of toxic stuff. We're all connected.

Well, I guess what I mean is that this beach is no worse now than anyplace else. He paused and looked back at Late Louise. *Besides, I think she's going to nest high enough so we don't have to worry. And we need to get back.*

They were home before dawn.

"Are you sure?" Liberty was on the telephone with a member of the Keys Wildlife Guardians. "So it wouldn't be for several days until you could send someone over?" She made a worried face and looked at July, who was standing beside her. "Yeah, yeah, I know it's the end of the season . . . okay. Thanks." She hung up the phone.

"Bad news?" July asked.

"Well, not really bad bad news, but they said that there are other keys with bigger populations of turtles, not just leatherbacks, but hawksbills and some other kinds, too. Those keys need help more, because they have poachers over there who steal the eggs, and all sorts of things. They are just too busy and understaffed to get over to our key." Liberty paused. "They think the season is just about over, anyhow."

"Well, we tried," July said.

13

Color It Purple

IS THIS *a coincidence or what?* Liberty tele-alarmed across the breakfast table two days later.

July opened his eyes so wide they seemed like immense gray pools. Had he heard his father right? "What did you say, Dad?"

"Diploidymysterol—a horribly toxic substance, but big money in getting rid of it."

"Really?" Zanny said.

"How terrible!" said Madeline, who was down for the week. "What does it do?"

"And what is it used for?" Zanny asked.

The older twins were utterly speechless, their telepathic channels stunned into silence.

"It's an all-purpose substance, I'll say that. Its base, diploid myst, is used for making solvents that scrub out oil tankers' storage tanks. It is also used for making blueprints. It has been used in chemical warfare, insect control, before new laws were passed, even paint removal—you name it. It's a bad item and number one on our most-wanted list, along with the thugs who dump it."

I can't believe I'm hearing this!

"Even minimal contact with it can be harmful. It leaves deep purple blisters, indistinguishable from burns. I have some literature on it in my desk. Quite frightening."

Liberty and July both sneaked a look at their hands. They appeared tan and a bit crinkly from so much time in the saltwater. Nothing purple.

Should we tell Dad, or what?

How can we tell him? If we say anything we have to also tell him we've gone out at night. Besides, that drum just drifted into Lonely Key, I'm sure. It wasn't put right there by anybody. It came with the tides and the currents. You know those are strong currents that run between Lonely and Sandy Key.

Yeah, I guess you're right, but . . .

But what, Liberty?

Well, maybe we should just keep our eyes open when we're around there. But I've never seen any boats that looked as if they were dumping anything.

Me, neither.

"What are you two so quiet about this morning?" Madeline asked. "Are you sure you're getting enough sleep?"

"Oh, definitely," Liberty replied. "And Mom,

please ask Charly and Molly not to bring Pinky to the breakfast table."

"Oh, dear, yes!" Madeline said as her eyes fixed on Pinky running up the outside of the clear glass orange-juice pitcher.

"Look, she's turning orange!" Charly exclaimed.

"Not too far from pink, Pinky. I'll bet you'll do it in another week, sweetie!" Molly cooed and extended her hand, which had purple press-on nails on the fingers. "Come here, cutie pie." Pinky ran straight up her hand, trotted across her wrist to her forearm, past her elbow, and took a straight shot to her shoulder. She proceeded up Molly's neck, heading for her ear.

"No living jewelry at the breakfast table!" Put said firmly.

Pinky must have heard him. She raced for Molly's hair and turned copper.

"This is so gross!" groaned July.

"Shut up, J. B.," Charly growled.

"Yeah, shut up!" Molly said.

"Shut up yourself!"

A full-fledged fight was breaking out.

Good going, J. B. It's a diversion from the sleep discussion.

We heard that! Charly teleblasted.

If you guys don't shut up, we'll tell Mom and Dad you look sleepy! Molly threatened.

Just keep quiet, you little sun-ripened pig droppings, or we'll tell Mom about how you let Pinky practice changing colors in that rainbow-print nightgown of hers.

You wouldn't dare.

Wouldn't we? Just try us, Liberty challenged.

"Are you children having a little discussion?" Put inquired, looking over the top of his reading glasses. Although Put had no way of entering into the telepathic channels, he could usually tell when the children were having a discussion, especially when it was as intense as this one. The silence alone was the giveaway.

"No!" they all said at once.

"Hmmph!" Putnam said. He scrutinized the four faces, then snapped his newspaper shut and got up from the table on the deck of the *Flagrant Flamingo*. "Well, I have to get to work—where are my thongs and briefcase?"

No, I don't believe it!

He saw us staring. I just know it.

But Liberty, his hands were the same color as that grape snow cone he was eating!

They were purple.

They were as purple as could be.

They were as purple as Aunt Honey's eyeshadow.

They were as purple as Molly and Charly's press-on nails.

They were, in a word, J. B., as purple as diploidy-mysterol! Liberty paused. *And to think I was worried about his fingers being melted together or webbed.*

It was not three hours later, and the twins were down at the Grubby Duck buying snow cones when they had encountered Robbie. His bandages had been removed the day before, and while everyone else in the Grubby Duck was fussing over his hands and saying how well they had healed and asking if he had learned his lesson about matches, Liberty and July were struck dumb by the bright purple of his skin—precisely what Putnam had described as the effects of the awful toxin diploidymysterol.

And Robbie, through his slitty eyes, had seen them staring and had felt them wondering. They just knew it. When they left the store they had sensed his eyes following them, and even now, as they turned down the sandy palmetto-fringed path that led to Pirate's Cove, they felt someone watching them. Suddenly July streaked through the thickest palm fronds.

"Gotcha!" he cried.

"Stop it! Stop it! Let me go!" the small hoarse voice yelled. It happened so fast that Liberty was taken totally by surprise. One minute July had been walking right beside her, and the next minute he had plunged into the lush, jungle growth. Now he emerged, and all she could see were these two bright purple hands furiously flailing at the air. But July was much bigger and had effectively collared him.

"I'm not going to hurt you. I just want to see your hands."

"July, that's rude!" Liberty blurted out. "He's a special needs child!" She clamped her hands over her mouth, but it was too late. Then Robbie said a word—

a really dirty word. The kind of word their grandmother said was the wash-your-mouth-out-with-soap kind of word. Somehow he broke loose from July and tore back into the trees.

"I got a good look at those hands." July was breathing heavily. "They are weird and definitely purple. We have to get that stuff out of Dad's desk and read about this."

A half hour later, July and Liberty were poring over articles on diploidymysterol that they had found in their father's desk. Many of them were very scientific and used big words that neither of them knew.

But a picture is worth a thousand words, July flashed, and swung out of his hammock. *Look at this!*

It was a color picture of some hands that had come into contact with the toxin. Except for their size, the hands looked exactly like Robbie's.

And do you see those little crinkly ridges—so regular, kind of like corduroy?

Yeah.

They say that anything with diploid myst does that to skin—a subtle difference between that and regular burns, but one that your average physician might not pick up on.

Yeah?

Well, I got a close-up look at Robbie's hands—they had those ridges.

And they took him to a clinic on the mainland.

You guessed it—your average physicians, no burn experts.

Jeez, I guess this is proof.

Sherlock Holmes would say incontrovertible proof.

He would say the game is afoot.

I would say the game is a hand!

14

A Surprise
in the Night

JULY AND LIBERTY could not get the turtles of Lonely Key out of their minds. As July had said after they spoke to the Keys Wildlife Guardians—they had tried. But the Guardians could not come to help them. So they had to do what they could just one more time.

The moonlight glistened on the metal of the slide, and there were two soft swooshes in the night, punctuated by the barely audible "plip" sound as each twin slipped into the still dark waters. They had become experts at soundlessly leaving the houseboat in the middle of the night. They swam to the *Little Coconut* and put their plastic bags of gear over the gunwales.

July was still holding on to the side of the boat, and Liberty had crawled into it, when he heard her say, "What? What are you doing here?"

Why was she speaking out loud? *What's happening?* July flashed. But his transmission fell into a void. Liberty looked straight over the side, her gray eyes bright and incredulous.

"He's here!"

"Who's here?"

"Robbie!"

"What?"

"Ssshh!" *We'll wake the whole boat.* She suddenly switched to the telepathic channels.

July hauled himself into the *Little Coconut.* Sure enough, there on the floorboards of the boat sat Robbie. Even in the darkness J. B. could see the purple tinge of his scarred hands.

Why is he here?

How long has he been here?

Questions flew through the air as thick and annoying as the little no-see-ums that ruled the tropical air and drove people to itching distraction. And although Robbie could not enter into the telepathic channels, one did not have to be telepathic to guess what questions were flooding the twins' minds. He knew he had thrown them into a tailspin, and this was exactly what he had intended.

Robbie knew a lot about Liberty and July. They had real parents, even though their mom only came in every week or so. They were a weird family, though. It was like seeing double. That was why he first started shadowing them, following them around.

Robbie stared silently through his half-closed eyes, watching them try to make sense out of him being there.

Liberty looked at Robbie huddled silently on the floorboards, utterly motionless, the eyes still only half opened. She soon realized that it wasn't that his face seemed like a mask so much as his features seemed so small and expressionless. It was as if they were stranded on his face.

"What are you doing here?" Liberty hissed.

"Sssh!" July said. "We'll wake everybody up. Wait a second." He untied the boat and began poling it out of the cove. When they were well clear of the houseboat, July put down the oar he was poling with. He stared straight at Robbie.

"Okay—explain yourself," he demanded.

"Me explain myself!" The little slit-eyes opened wide at last. "Listen, buster, you and your sister are the ones that have the explaining to do."

Well, I'll give him credit for guts—gutsy response there, Liberty flashed.

Obnoxious, that's what I call it—the nerve!

I feel kind of sorry for him, J. B.

"Hey, you weirdos, what are you doing?" Robbie could tell that something was going on that didn't include him. It felt as if they were talking about him behind his back; but here he was, right in front of them, and he couldn't hear anything except the sound of the wind in the palmettos.

"Why do we have to explain ourselves?" July asked.

"I saw you go out twice, out the channel 'round the back side of Sook's Key, then head out toward Sandy Key."

"So?" said Liberty.

"So I want to go."

Liberty and July looked at each other.

What can we do?

I guess we could use an extra pair of hands—purple hands—to transfer eggs and get the hatchlings down to the water.

If we don't take him, he'll probably go tell on us.

Maybe . . . but . . . July broke off his thought and continued aloud.

"Maybe you should tell us how you got those purple hands of yours—it wasn't fire, was it?"

Robbie was stunned. Not even the doctors knew what happened to his hands. His heart was beating so loud and furiously he thought it would burst. If anybody found out . . . Robbie could not bear to think, but he knew he'd be dead.

"So what about your hands?"

Robbie became mute, his eyes slits once again.

"So?" said Liberty.

"It's none of your business," Robbie said.

"Yes it is," July persisted. "You got that from messing with diploidymysterol."

"I don't know what you're talking about." He was right. He didn't know what they were talking about.

He's not going to talk, J. B. It's no use. We're stuck with him—for better or for worse.

You make it sound like we're getting married to him. Next thing you're going to say is for richer or for poorer.

Liberty didn't think of it as marriage, but she suddenly saw that behind the mask, behind those half-mast eyes, there might be somebody home. She made a decision right then.

"Okay, Robbie," she said. "You want to know what we're doing?"

"Yeah."

"We're saving turtles."

"Saving turtles?" he asked with wonder.

"Yep. We go out to Lonely Key. It's just beyond Sandy Key and there's a beach there where leatherback turtles come to lay their eggs. We help them, and we help others—little ones that hatch—get down to the water before the crabs grab them up and eat them."

Robbie tucked his chin. "Can I help?" It was as if his tongue were now bandaged instead of his hands, and he had to force the words out.

"You're actually asking?" July said, stunned by his sudden politeness.

"It's better than Parcheesi."

"What does Parcheesi have to do with anything?" Liberty asked.

"Bert and Mabel play Parcheesi, and I'm sick of it."

"Well, okay," Liberty said. "You can come along, but you have to swear not to tell anybody."

Robbie bit his lip lightly as if contemplating this

demand. But Liberty knew what he was really thinking. Can I trust them? Are they going to make me tell my secret? She knew they had his confidence, but at a terrible price—a price they all might pay for some day, with more than just purple hands.

15

An Ocean to Grow In

DESPITE HIS STIFF HANDS, Robbie proved amazingly quick and nimble in picking up the hatchlings and the turtle eggs. He rarely talked, and Liberty and July still felt as if they had an observer along rather than a companion.

They had just about finished getting the last of the hatchlings down to the surf and were wading up to the beach. Robbie was sitting on the sand with his hands cupped. The little flippers of a baby turtle flailed within the cage of his purple fingers. "Don't worry," he was whispering. "I'll take care of you." He popped the baby into his shirt pocket.

"Are you crazy!"

"Stop that!" Liberty and July were both screaming.

"Don't you understand anything?" Liberty gasped. "That turtle will die if you take it home. The whole point is to get it to the sea."

"I'll make a little pool for it. He'll be fine." Robbie

was holding his hand over his shirt pocket, and inside it the little turtle was bucking. It looked almost as if Robbie's heart was pulsing madly, so madly that it would break through his body. "I can take care of it. I'm good. I know how to take care of things."

Liberty's eyes were fixed on the frantic little movements in his shirt pocket. She wanted to cry.

This is sad! July flashed.

I can't help but think of breaking hearts. Look at his shirt pocket, how it's jumping around.

We can't let him do it, Liberty. It'll die.

Not to mention that if it doesn't die, Mabel and Bert might not like a one-thousand-pound turtle crawling around their yard.

"Robbie," Liberty said in a soft voice. "We know you would never hurt it on purpose. And I know you'd try to take good care of it. But there are certain things humans just can't take care of. It's a turtle, and you're human. And it needs to be in the water with its kind, and . . . and . . ." She hesitated. "You need to be on land with humans. And it will die if it doesn't have an ocean to grow in."

"You saw the mothers, Robbie," July was saying. "They can grow to weigh more than a thousand pounds. They can't do that at Mabel and Bert's, no matter how nice you make the pool."

Robbie looked up at the twins. He opened his eyes so wide they were no longer slits at all, but looked round and shiny in the moonlight. Nobody had ever talked to him this way. People had told him what to do and what not to do, but nobody had told him he needed . . . how had they said it . . . to be on land with humans. It was as if they were saying there was this place waiting for him, not a foster home, but a place where he belonged on this earth.

"I guess you're right," he said in a small, rough voice.

"Come on," July said. "I'll give you a hand."

"Yeah," Liberty said. "I'll watch out for the crabs, and you and July take him in right there, where the surf runs back smoothly." She pointed to a spot down the beach, a little to the left of where they were standing.

The three children walked down to the surf. Robbie had taken the turtle out of his pocket and was holding it in his hands. Liberty kept a sharp eye out for crabs, but there wasn't really any need since Robbie was carrying the baby right to the water. They waded in a few feet until the water swirled about their ankles.

Robbie brought his hands close to his face. "Okay, little buddy," he whispered. Then he bent over. Liberty and July watched as he sunk his hands just beneath the surface. For one dreadful, unspeakable second they feared Robbie might not release the turtle. But he did. The turtle paddled off into the surf. What waited just beyond—a shark? A barracuda?

It was as if Robbie were reading their thoughts. "Hope nothing gets it out there."

July felt he had to say something hopeful, even though he knew the odds were not great. He had read that only one hatchling out of one thousand makes it to maturity. "Well, you saw how that little guy's belly was white."

"Yeah," said Robbie.

"That helps fool the sharks and anything underneath it. They look up and think it's part of the sky."

"Yeah." Liberty spoke now. "And its back is dark so when birds look down they think it's part of the water."

"Pretty smart," Robbie said.

"Yep," both twins said at once.

They started home in the *Little Coconut* under a light breeze. Liberty was at the tiller, and July handled the sheets, or ropes, that controlled the sails. They had hoped they might be able to get Robbie to talk a little more. They wondered if they could ever ask him about his hands and where he had come in contact with the diploidymysterol.

But Robbie just sat in the bottom of the boat, staring over the side into the phosphorescent water. Every now and then he would trail his hand for a few minutes, as if waving a very long good-bye to the little turtle he had just released.

16

Shark Bite
In The Night

THE *LITTLE COCONUT* had just come out of the channel between Lonely Key and Sandy Key when the twins and Robbie heard the putt-putt of the engine of another boat. The hull of a speedboat suddenly loomed out of the dark, moonless night. Robbie slammed himself against the floorboards of the boat.

"What are you doing?" Liberty yelled.

Robbie had pulled a sail bag over himself and crawled right into it. "Get us out of here! Fast!" He spat the words. But there was no getting out fast. Their sail was up. They would have to lower the sail and start the engine, and it usually took three times for either July or Liberty to get the engine started. The big boat was gliding up to them now at idling speed. The hull hung over the *Little Coconut* like the jaws of an enormous beast about to swallow them.

I think I know how Jonah must have felt when he met the whale, July flashed.

Who are these guys?

Nobody Robbie wanted to meet.

A voice cracked the still, dark night.

"Whatcha doin? Fishing?"

These guys aren't fishing. Why should we be? Liberty flashed.

The man peered down. "You out here alone?" he yelled over the sound of the engine.

July wished they would move off. It wasn't easy to sail the *Little Coconut* with such a big boat chopping up the calm waters and blanketing the already light wind. The man didn't wait for an answer. He quickly took in the whole picture, which wasn't a large one given that the *Little Coconut* was only ten feet long and barely four feet across. "Hey, Cuda. It's just kids!" On the word "Cuda," Liberty saw the sail bag flinch.

J. B., these are the guys!

What guys?

These are the diploidymysterol guys.

It was clear now to Liberty why Robbie was hiding in the bottom of the boat. But there was no way July could have known. He was at the tiller and had not seen that flinch in the sail bag. The name "Cuda" had gone through Robbie like an electrical current.

"Oh yeah!" Liberty said, pumping a carefree, cheerful-as-a-kid-in-a-candy-store note into her voice. "We're fishing and doing our nighttime solo navigation trip. Well, not exactly solo. You do it in pairs. It's this scouting badge we're working on."

July didn't know what was happening. Liberty was

blabbing a mile a minute, but something warned him that he'd better fall in with it. The something that warned him was Liberty's telepathic voice. This was difficult for her to do—talk in two voices at once—aloud to the grown-ups and telepathically to her twin. Things got garbled and staticky; messages on the telepathic level broke up. It was like trying to pat your head and rub your stomach at the same time, only ten times harder.

"Well, you better scout right on out of here." Another man had come up to the bow of the boat. He was tall and bony. Even in the darkness Liberty could see that his skin seemed to fit too tight on his body, which gave him a skeletal look. "Y'understand?" He grinned. His thin lips stretched into a smile made jagged by missing teeth. The teeth he had were glistening and pointed.

The guy looks just like a barracuda, July teleflashed. *Let's get out of here.*

They sailed out from under the shadow of the boat's prow. Liberty winced as she looked up and saw the name of the boat written in letters almost a foot high. *Shark Bite.*

When they were good and clear, Liberty lowered the sail and July started the engine. Thankfully, it started on the second try. Liberty leaned over the sail bag. "You can come out now, Robbie."

When they cut into the channel leading to Pirate's Cove, July shut down the engine.

Okay, Liberty. It's no more Mr. Nice Guy. Robbie really has some explaining to do. Who's going to put it to him?

I will, she said.

Robbie was sitting hunched over in the bottom of the boat with the sail bag still wrapped partway around him.

"Who is Cuda, Robbie?"

Silence.

"Robbie, you have to tell us. Who is this guy?"

More silence.

Trying a different approach, July said, "Robbie, Cuda is the guy with the stuff that messed up your hands, isn't he?"

Robbie did not stir. Liberty could hardly detect him breathing. Shock tactics were in order. Liberty had been the patient one with Robbie, the one to give him the benefit of the doubt. But it was time for a switch.

"Look Robbie, I'm not your social worker, and I don't care what you think or do, but you're a hypocrite if you won't 'fess up about all this stuff, because your hands are small potatoes next to what this poison could do to the whole earth. Think about that baby turtle. You got him to the surf, and then with any kind of luck he'll swim out to the ocean, and maybe there's a shark waiting, but maybe the shark will look up and see that white belly and say, 'Uh, duh, that's just a little piece of sky flipping by.' "

Though she didn't know what a talking shark

sounded like, Liberty was fairly convincing. "And then maybe this bird flies over and sees the turtle's dark back, or doesn't see it, and just says, 'Uh, water, just water down there, nothing to eat.' So now he's free and clear on his first day of life, and the sun comes up, and just as he's swimming into the morning, he hits a leaking can of diploidymysterol, and one, two, three, he's a jellified blob of turtle meat."

Liberty paused. There was not even a flicker of feeling on Robbie's face.

The next morning, Robbie was gone. Word was all over Pelican Key. Bert and Mabel's foster kid had taken off.

17

A Hot, Endless Day

"I MEAN, I thought he was happy." Mabel was wiping her eyes down at the Grubby Duck. Her nose was bright red, and her hand shook as she raised her coffee cup. "Or 'bout as happy as Robbie gets. You never can tell with a kid like that. And yeah, sure it was a strain on us, not being so young and all. But I think we were helping the boy, I do." She sighed deeply. It reminded Liberty and July of the gasping mother turtles on the beach crying their huge, thick tears.

"Don't go blaming yourself, dear," Ally said.

The worst part is we have to pretend we didn't know him.

Yeah. If they found out what we did . . . July didn't finish the thought.

And don't you kind of feel as if everyone's saying we should have been nicer to him?

Sure enough, Mabel turned to them and said, "I wish you children could've gotten to know Robbie. It's been so hard for him. He's just been moved from place to place for most of his life—I don't think he ever felt like he had a real home. He's gotten into some trouble before—vandalism at his last foster home—but we really hoped he'd like it here with us. I know he was a little standoffish, but I think he could have warmed up."

A little standoffish! What an understatement.

Oh, I'm feeling rotten. Gee whiz, we can't even say he was getting to be our friend . . . July paused. *In a way, I guess we'll never really know if he thought of us as his friends or not.*

Liberty knew what July meant. She recalled the narrow slit eyes and remembered how she had wondered if anyone was home behind them. But last night on the beach when he had tried to hold onto the baby turtle, those same eyes had opened up round and wide with a kind of astonishment when they had told Robbie . . . She stopped and tried to think exactly what they had said to him last night. How had they put it?

He needed to be on land with humans, July teleflashed.

Yes. Liberty remembered that look in his eyes as if it were the first time anybody had told him he belonged on this planet, had a special place on this earth—with people.

What were they to do? The day dragged on hot and endless. Tempers were short, and every hour or so they wanted to walk down to the Grubby Duck to find out any news. Zanny was becoming increasingly irritated, too. None of the twins were concentrating on their schoolwork. But it was hard to think about base ten math problems, or even the gold route that had taken the Spanish mariners across the Gulf of Mexico.

"And you see, kids," Zanny was saying, "the reason there were so many shipwrecks around here is that the Spaniards, for all their navigational know-how and smarts, had no method of measuring longitude. They could measure latitude but not longitude, and because of this they did not like to be out of the sight of land. If they hugged the coral chain, as they called it, the string of small islands which were the Keys, they felt a lot better, but it was very dangerous, too, because they could run into the big coral heads and wreck their ships. So . . ."

She stopped abruptly. Her bright green eyes turned cold. "You guys aren't even listening to me. I am trying my darndest, and you're not paying any attention."

A child is lost, and she thinks we should be glued to her lecture on Spanish gold and greed, July flashed.

I know. It could just make you throw up.

"Look kids, I know you're upset about this little boy, but honestly, you never really gave him the time of day before. He was a troubled youth. It wasn't like he was your best friend."

Gads, she sounds so . . . so . . .

Zanny finished the thought for them, though she wasn't telepathic. "So grown-up, so insensitive. You're right." She plopped down in a chair. It was no use trying to teach these kids anything more today. They weren't going to concentrate. They were too upset about Robbie, even though they hardly knew him.

"Look, I know this is tough," she said. "It's scary thinking of a little kid just running off, all alone."

"Maybe they'll put his picture on a milk carton," Charly chimed in.

Zanny bit her lip lightly. All the twins recognized the gesture. Nine times out of ten it signaled that a big idea was brewing in Zanny's head. "I don't know about a milk carton, but I just had a thought."

"Yeah?" Liberty and July both asked at once.

"Why don't we get a picture of Robbie from Mabel and Bert? We can get photocopies made on the mainland and spend the rest of the day putting fliers up between here and Key West."

Liberty and July put up the last flier outside a juice bar on Duval Street in Key West and bought themselves their favorite tropical drink, made with pineapple juice and coconut cream. They were to meet Zanny and the little twins in another fifteen minutes in Mallory Square, at the spot where the tightrope walker set up his show.

Mallory Square was like a circus without a tent. There were jugglers and acrobats, trinket traps and junk food, fire eaters, and generally an amazing collection of people ranging from slightly bewildered tourists to mahogany-tanned beach weirdos. But it all became tiresome if this was your fifth or sixth visit, as it was for July and Liberty, and if your mind was on something else. So the children, with a few minutes to spare, began to wander along the waterfront.

Boats of all kinds were docked there—little ten-horsepower fishing dories, big cruise ships at one end, dive boats that took people out to the reef to scuba dive or snorkle. Suddenly Liberty grabbed July's arm.

Look there! she teleflashed.

Where? Oh, there!

It's Cuda.

Instinctively the twins fell into the shadows behind two very large tourists. The tourists had planted themselves solidly on the walkway between the pier and where the twins were standing. They were admiring the view, the sunset, and the bright little boats bobbing on the glittering turquoise water, as they ate Belgian waffles dripping with ice cream.

The sun, the color of molten gold, was squashing down on the horizon like the yolk of an immense egg, and the sound of cameras whirring and clicking was as thick as peepers in a swamp. But Liberty and July could not have cared less about the sunset. They were peeking around the bulging contours of the couple in front, who were dressed in matching prints of palms trees and hibiscus. The man wore a shirt and shorts and the lady a muumuu. She held her half-eaten Belgian waffle in one hand and rested her free hand on her ample hip.

Liberty had a clear view through the crook of the woman's elbow, and she could see Cuda on the dock. He was loading empty drums onto the stern of the boat. Once more Liberty winced as she saw the words *Shark Bite*.

What are those other guys doing? July flashed.

I don't know.

The twins watched as two more men began lowering a large crate onto the boat.

"Okay, easy does it." Cuda's voice cut straight through the whirr of tourists' cameras and the festival-like din of Mallory Square. There was no sunset, no icky food, no jugglers. There was only the flash of those strangely pointed teeth as Liberty and July cowered behind the two tourists.

18

This Is Not a Dream

THE TURTLE EGG-LAYING SEASON was over. From the tiny little flipper tracks they found on the beach, Liberty and July could tell that the last of the hatchlings had come out the evening after Robbie disappeared, which had been four days before. Still there was no sign of him. But July and Liberty, out of habit or some undefinable urge, were still drawn to the beach of Lonely Key each day after their lessons.

They were not sure what they were looking for now. A last little hatchling, a late bloomer that would need their help down to the shore? A very, very Late Louise who had laid her eggs much too close to the tideline? A glimpse, perhaps, of the *Shark Bite* plying the Gulf waters with its empty drums? Oh yes, their minds had been feverish with thoughts of what those empty drums had once contained. Or maybe—hope against hope—were they waiting for Robbie?

Had he, like the little hatchlings, left on a rising tide to join the very creatures he had wanted to hold on to? Would he, after years of wandering, find a warm, familiar current that would tug him back to a dim beach in his memory, an early first shore? To July and Liberty, Robbie seemed as homeless, as motherless, and as hopelessly adrift as those young hatchlings. It made no sense that Robbie would come to Lonely Key, but still they went and waited.

And then one night, while swinging in their hammocks, July and Liberty began to hear more than just the squeak of the ropes. There were clicks, muffled, but nonetheless there—clicks somewhere deep in their brains, calling them. They had to go. They slipped out of the houseboat and returned to Lonely Key.

On this night there was not a breath of wind, and the water, like a dark mirror, held the reflections of stars quivering on its surface. The children dug their toes into the still-warm sand and listened to the lapping of the surf, their minds entranced by shadows and sparkles, water sounds and stars that seemed as still and smooth as the ocean they gazed out upon.

The world seemed infinite. The rhythms of the sea, the gentle swells farther out, the upwellings, the ebb and flow of tides, all seemed to find a harmony within the twins' own human rhythms. Did their hearts actually slow, their pulse beats synchronize to these eternal sea sounds? Were they rocked by the oldest music of the earth?

July's and Liberty's eyes became increasingly accustomed to the night, and they were soon able to pick out features in the darkness of the ocean. The water, instead of being simply black and smooth, became a lambent, deep blue-black, seemingly calm, yet pulsing with life. And from that still blue-black sea there came sudden glints, as if the stars had smashed and scattered. The twins blinked, then blinked again. Their breath caught in their throats.

This is not a dream!

They stood up. The glints laced the water. Sleek and silver, they came closer and closer to the shore.

No, it's not! July, I can't believe it! Liberty tele-whispered. *They have come! They have finally come . . .* She paused. *They have come for us, July!*

Click . . . click-click.

The sound, once deep in their brains, was still within their heads, but crisper and louder. Liberty was right. The dolphins had come back for them.

The twins waded into the surf, the same surf where they had released the young hatchlings. They pushed through the breaking waves. The foam swirled around their knees and then their waists. They gave no thought to any danger beyond the surf line. They knew there was none, for only the dolphins were waiting.

There were six of them. Sleek and strong, fast and graceful, they cut through the water just beneath the surface and then began leaping. Silver arcs in the moonlight curved out of the sea.

July and Liberty felt their feet leave the sandy bottom as water tugged at their clothes. They felt themselves suspended in the dark blue infinity beneath them, cradled by the swells and rocking of the water.

The sea appeared braided by the swift, silvery shapes of the dolphins. They were swimming a tangled circle around the children, filling the dark blue emptiness with their presence, their curiosity, their gentleness. Clicks laced the air as well as the water and swirled within the children's heads. There were long riffs of clicks like musical phrases, and embedded within them the children sensed meaning.

The meaning was felt but not easily translated. There was a message. Both children felt it so strongly that they dove down together as if to grasp the sense of it all. As they dove, they swam out of their shorts and jackets. Down they plunged through the water, wearing just their underwear.

> *Come . . . come.* The clicks pulled at their minds. *Join us!*

Their eyes were open, and out of the darkness of the water, like the first stars of the night, legions of white spots swirled around them. The stars would beam in on them and then shoot off.

It's their noses. It's the white tips of their noses, July flashed. They seemed to be traveling within a galaxy of dolphins. It was impossible to count how many, for the dolphins swam around them so fast. They skimmed so close that Liberty and July could feel their own bodies tingle, and the little bursts of clicks seemed to resonate through their every bone.

The twins did not know how long they had been

underwater. It could not have been more than half a minute, for at the first twinge of a shortness of breath four dolphins swam up and offered their dorsal fins, one on each side of each twin. July and Liberty grabbed hold, and the four sleek animals brought them to the surface. One dolphin from each pair then dove again, but the twins were left each holding a dorsal fin of the remaining two dolphins. These two rolled slightly, seeming to cue the children to straddle their backs.

Liberty felt the dolphin's silky skin now against her own bare legs. A light breeze riffled the water, breaking the reflected starlight into a million fragments. Her eyes stung from the salt. She looked across at July. With his legs slung across the dolphin's midsection, he crouched low like a jockey. His hair was slicked straight back, and his face was still wet but sparkling in the moonlight.

The thunder of their hearts seemed for a moment to muffle the clicks of the dolphins. But soon both July and Liberty began to notice that the clicks were interspersed with longer whistles. And they listened hard, sensing, though not able to pinpoint exactly, a kind of message or meaning every now and again.

As they cruised through the water, the dolphins stayed inches beneath the surface, but Liberty and July rode with their heads and shoulders well above it. Occasionally the animals broke through the surface to sound with a spurt from their blowholes.

Gradually meaning came. It came not with any

particular sound or rhythm or syllable, and not as a whole word or phrase, but nonetheless the clicks and whistles began to make sense. Like a shape or a holographic picture, the messages suspended themselves in their minds, to be read, to be decoded or encoded. Soon it seemed to be happening within the telepathic channels, and the children were barely aware of the audible sounds at all. It felt as if they had been talking Dolphin all their lives.

> *Delphinese. That's what the scientists call our language.*
>
> *But they don't really listen. They are mostly interested in teaching us their kinds of signaling. Isn't that true, Eelhyrr?*

What? July asked. *I didn't quite catch the end of that.*

> *Don't worry. That's my cousin's name. It roughly translates to Spray. Just call him Spray, and call me Crest. What are your names?*

July.
Liberty.

> *Odd.*

Liberty was itching to ask Spray and Crest a million questions, but she was not sure how to go about it or which ones to ask first. She sensed that perhaps it was better to let them do the talking for now. Hadn't Crest said that the scientists were always teaching them their own kinds of signaling? Maybe she and July should just wait a bit and listen. Their father always said you learned more by listening than by talking.

> *Look at Vyshiniylrr, or Streak.* Crest seemed to have tuned into Liberty's thoughts, to her continued amazement. *Streak is that dolphin swimming off the near fluke of Spray. See that notch in her flipper? I'll dive so you can get a better look. Hang on!*

Down they went through a slide of bubbles. Soon they were skimming so close to Streak that Liberty thought they would collide or that the other dolphin's tail might accidentally slap them with one of the powerful strokes that propelled the animal through the water.

> *Don't worry.*

And suddenly she knew it had been foolish to worry the least bit. The sound picture that filled the dolphin's brain became complete and radiant in her own. She knew precisely the curve and shape of every pressure wave created by Crest and all the dolphins swimming about them. She felt as if she could actually see the currents of the water, the shape of the wake they left behind them, the pattern of the waves flowing about them.

Liberty was receiving a three-dimensional sound

picture of amazing detail and intensity. It was as if her own brain, until this moment, had been playing at a very slow speed. By comparison to this sound world of dolphins, the other world seemed dull, lifeless, and without color. Liberty wondered if this was how a blind person who suddenly gained sight would feel—whose eyes were finally opened to a new world of color, shape, and contour. Yes, she saw the notch now in Streak's flipper. It was white and crisscrossed with tiny lines as opposed to the dark velvety gray of the rest of the flipper.

> *They put a transmitter on her. Finally we got it off.*

> *I was ready to cruise up to a shark and offer a nip to get rid of the darned thing.*

Streak swam very close, rolled slightly, and fixed Liberty with a lovely big eye, so gentle and full of humor that Liberty felt herself brim with joy. Then her breath ran short.

> *Take her to the top!* Streak clicked, rolled, and offered a dorsal fin. *Let me help, too!*

Liberty slid off Crest but still hung onto his dorsal fin with one hand, and with her other, she reached for Streak's dorsal. She flew through the sea as foils of water billowed under her body. She felt the shape of their flukes sculpting the wake behind them as they raced her to the surface.

How do you always know just when to get me up to air? I barely think it, and you know to do it.

Yeah, good question, flashed July, who had just surfaced on Spray.

> *We sense these things,* said Crest. *It's part of the sound picture you send out. Your heart rhythms and pulses change. We know it's time. That's all.*

That's all! It didn't seem that was all to the twins. It seemed very complicated. The world of the dolphins was hugely complex. The animals could take in more information at higher rates of speed than was imaginable for humans. The dolphins seemed to live in a symphony of color, shape, rhythm, sound, and speed.

So what happened with the transmitter? What was it for? Liberty asked.

> *To see . . .* Streak paused, and there was almost a gleeful glimmer in the water surrounding them, *how the best of the best swims!*

And with that, Streak shot straight down. There was an inverted cone of bubbles below, and in the center was a glistening stream of light. Streak broke through the water and leaped into the starry night. Liberty and July held their breaths as they saw the dolphin arc toward the moon, then plunge back down again. But the show was not over. Streak swam through the Gulf at speeds so high that the animal was only a streak of light in the night waters, skimming close, veering off, plunging, turning.

Two minutes later, Streak was cruising between Liberty on Crest and July on Spray.

> *That's what they wanted to know about. That was the reason for the monitor. To them I was Dolphin Number 23, swimming south by southeast in the Gulf. On their computers they would see that I had just surfaced from my second dive within an hour, a dive that lasted seven minutes. I had gone to a depth of five-hundred-twenty feet where the temperature was forty-one degrees. More important, they realized I could go faster and deeper than many dolphins. They wanted me.*

They? asked Liberty.

The Navy.

What for? July asked.

> *Hydrodynamic testing. We are, you know, the perfect shape for speed.*

Streak rolled over. Again the water seemed to glimmer with the dolphins' cheerfulness. Crest and Spray glimmered, too. And both Liberty and July felt a tingle run through them as they grasped the dolphins' backs. Oddly enough, there was nothing boastful about the way the dolphins rejoiced in their abilities to swim and their beauty. If anything, they wanted to share themselves with the children—but not the Navy.

Streak, continued Crest, *was the best swimmer, in this ocean at least.*

I have a cousin, Streak said, *in the Indian Ocean. Haven't seen her in years, but she is something to behold. They say that even the spinner dolphins are impressed by her leaps.*

In any case, the Navy wanted Streak, so they caught her one day off Gold Key, put a transmitter on her, and decided indeed she was for them.

Study me and you get the optimum design for a torpedo. Measure the shape, the flow, the pressure of the water around my body when I am swimming, and you begin to understand hydroplaning and hydrodynamics and everything else the Navy wanted to know for whatever it is they do.

July and Liberty both felt an uncomfortable twinge.

Don't worry, said Spray. *We know what the Navy does, and so does Streak. The Navy wanted to study us for war. We know the difference between a torpedo and a canoe.*

They weren't bad to me at all, interrupted Streak. *They were really quite wonderful. But it got so lonely swimming those endless patterns through their tanks. And my skin changed. It really did. I finally left and never came back. It was on an open sea run one day. They sometimes took me out of the tanks and had me do what they called open sea charges. Well, it was on one of those that I met up with Crest.*

Hardly recognized Streak. Her skin had become so dull in the tank.

And I wasn't swimming nearly as well, either. You see, these scientists would stand around and talk about the information they were getting from the transmitter they had on me. They'd talk about it while I was in the tank or when they were trans-porting me in the wet sling to the open water. And they were always talking about the laminar flow.

Laminar flow? Liberty repeated.

Yes, that's the nonturbulent flow of water across a body—mine in this case. Dolphins have very thin skin.

Very silky skin, said July.

Yes, possibly. Of course, silky is an idea that we don't really know since we don't wear clothes. But perhaps. See, this very thin skin, what the scientists call the epidermis, locks into an underneath layer through a system of small ridges. This makes the water flow perfectly around us, as we move through it with the least amount of resistance. But as my skin became dull, these ridges changed, and the lock between the outer or top layer and the underneath layer was not as fine.

They never noticed it, of course, but I did. The water felt different as I moved through it. I'm vain, I admit it, and when Crest said I looked so poor, well, I thought the next time he sees me I'll be swimming worse than ever, and he'll notice that. I knew I had to go. Eddie was my trainer. He was a Navy frogman. He had been wonderful to me, and I knew he would be upset, but you know, I think he understood when I didn't come back from that last open sea charge.

These children are getting cold. We'd better take them back to the beach.

Hammerhead! The image shrieked in July's brain.

Liberty turned her head and saw the bizarre T-shaped shadow, then the fin slicing through the water.

There was a sudden burst of clicks.

Don't worry. We can smash those fellows to bits, Spray said, and then, almost as an afterthought added, *but we can't always be around. So do be careful. We'll talk more about that next time.*

Next time!

19

To The Rescue

THERE WAS INDEED a next time. The following night the children fell asleep after gazing through the skylight at a moonless sky, black and without a star. Their sleep was as dreamless as the night was starless, but then, somewhere in the empty blackness of their sleep, both July and Liberty began to hear tiny clicks. They were as dim and muffled as if they'd been emitted from the farthest reaches of the universe, like those faint signals astronomers pick up from unknown stars billions of light years away.

A smothery feeling slipped over them like a thick, woolly blanket. Both twins woke violently at once, gasping in their hammocks. They gulped deep breaths of the night air.

We've got to go! J. B. flashed. *They're calling us!*

Liberty looked up through the stained-glass skylight. Now the stars had come out, and the Southern Cross appeared, more beautiful than every rose in the frame of the skylight, each of its four stars a different color through the tint of the skylight's panes. J. B. was right. They must go. Liberty knew the dolphins would be waiting.

The wind was perfect, and it did not take them long to get to the beach at Lonely Key. By the time Liberty and July waded into the water, the dolphins were swimming in silver circles. Once again the children climbed on the beautiful animals' backs and swam off in the moonlight. They had almost forgotten how luminous that world of shared images was. The picture-thoughts that suspended in all of their minds seemed more vivid than words, and far more powerful.

Although they didn't forget entirely about Robbie, for the first time their worry dulled. July was riding on Streak's back, and Liberty was on Spray's. Streak was recounting the story of a friend of hers who spent several weeks in a Dolphinarium near Key Largo, where captive dolphins were kept for the amusement of tourists.

> *Can you imagine having people pay to kiss you? The indignity of it all. How it does offend! They would actually line up to bend over the tank and kiss a dolphin—a dolphin who had been eating dead fish, so you can imagine the breath. Dead fish is, of course, the only kind you get in captivity. It's a terrible adjustment. I fasted for three days after the Navy caught me. But then I broke down and ate some of their stinking Spanish mackerel.*

The quicksilver images glinted between their minds. But Liberty, riding on Spray's back, sensed that Spray was in some way distracted, outside this aura of clicks and whistles. It seemed that almost as soon as Liberty perceived the first real glimmerings of Spray's distraction, Streak interrupted him.

> *I know, I know, you're worried about our dear Lunsyphrr.*

Moon Spirit? July asked.

> *Yes, you children are good with translation. No sign still, Spray?*

> *None . . . Crest has been out looking all day. We now think there is only one place she can be.*

Is this why we are here? Liberty asked, with a sudden, almost blinding flash of insight.

> *Oh my, you are quick,* Spray replied. *In a sense yes, but we needed you even before Moon Spirit disappeared.*

July interrupted this time. *That's why you first came to us, isn't it? That very first day you appeared in the bay when our dad was taking us all to Pelican Key. It's all part of the same thing, isn't it?*

There was nothing wasted in Delphinese communication. The meaning came with great bursts of insight and logic. Although there were no real descriptors in terms of adjectives or adverbs, it was all poetry in one sense, for it was a muscular language of verb pictures, silken with motion and rhythm.

We've been brought here, haven't we? Brought here to the Keys, July flashed.

Yes, replied Liberty, and she bent over on Spray's back until her chin rested tenderly just above the dolphin's jawline. She was remembering now the moonlit leaves on the branches of the elm tree back at their house in Washington, and how the oval leaves printed a shadowy design on her bedroom curtains, a design that had reminded her of fish, schools of swimming fish. But they were not really fish. They were dolphins, belonging to the order of mammals like themselves, perhaps family. Not perhaps—yes, family. She brushed her cheek lovingly against Spray's beautiful skin.

It wasn't like we just came here, July continued. *It's like in London when we were summoned.*

Yes, summoned.

Called.

Signaled.

The twins now realized this completely, and they also sensed they were approaching the heart of very mysterious and dangerous events.

> *Moon Spirit,* Spray began, and the watery world seemed to twinkle with the very name, *is a special and mysteriously beautiful dolphin. Many say she's the most beautiful dolphin in the sea. She is a pure white dolphin—they are rare, they are accidents, but beautiful.*

In your world, Streak continued, *she might be considered a freak. I heard about these freaks when I was around humans in the Navy Center. They call the white freaks albinos. But there are many kinds of freaks, and the human world often sets them apart and sometimes makes fun of them.*

July and Liberty knew about this. Within their own short lifetimes they had seen children made fun of, though not as often these days, not with all the emphasis on special education and children with special needs.

With needs! interrupted Streak. *You see, you think of these freaks as having needs. But we do not. We think of them as full and special and different.*

Exactly, continued Spray. *Moon Spirit does not lack color, not at all. Quite the reverse. She is white, so therefore she has all the colors of the spectrum.*

Of course, thought July, for when a white beam of light is broken up by passing through a prism, you have all the colors of the spectrum. *Moon Spirit must have it all and lack nothing in terms of color.*

Precisely, replied Spray. *And we common dolphins are by comparison pale, colorless shadows in the water. Moon Spirit comes from a long line of white dolphins. Her great-great-grandfather was Styllsphrr.*

Rainbow, Liberty translated.

> *Yes.* Spray explained that the last low whistle and click of the name was always the same for these white dolphins, for it meant "everything." *Everything, they lacked nothing. But now that is not so.*

What do you mean?

She swam too close to the bad-water place.

Diploidymysterol, July flashed. Then together both twins had the same thought. *Is she purple?*

> *Well, she has an odd purple tinge, but it is very pale, rather like the moon before the blackness of night settles in. But worse than that, this terrible poison has affected her brain. Moon Spirit was an animal of incredible sensitivity and delicacy. She could find schools of fish from distances that other dolphins could never sound for. Her sonar was exceptional. Next to Streak, she was the best swimmer in this region.*

> Streak interrupted. *She was not as fast perhaps, but she was equally beautiful, and her leaps were so delicate and intricate that when she came down the water splashed up in the most unforgettable designs. One of our favorite pastimes was watching Moon Spirit leap off Cobb's Reef, just beyond the shoals.*

And now? asked Liberty.

And now she is lost. Several times in the last few months she has nearly beached herself, for her sonar is in such bad condition. Her Delphinese has fal-tered. Often she cannot communicate at all. Two nights ago she almost beached herself again. We try to always have another dolphin swimming with her. Crest is the most attentive. Crest is particularly close to Moon Spirit, but he was not on duty today, and now Moon Spirit is lost.

Oh dear! Liberty sighed in Delphinese, and the sigh hung like mist in their brains.

We have a feeling, however, that she might have beached herself near Starfish Key. This is close to the bad water, and in the last few years the starfish themselves have begun to grow strange and twisted arms. If she is there, she will probably be on the southwestern side of the island, for that is the di-rection she was last swimming. This is the safest side of the island, where the starfish are still normal, Spray said.

But we need your help, and we need it now. If Moon Spirit has indeed beached herself, and I'm beginning to feel more and more strongly that she has, then she only has a few hours left on this tide. It is ebbing. Soon it will be dead low, and she will be beyond reach. Streak clicked these images with urgency.

You children are strong. If you can roll Moon Spirit down below the low tide mark and into just a bit of water, I think we can save her. We'll wait for you, but we cannot come in too shallow on this turning tide.

How far away is Starfish Key? July asked.

Not far. It is near the mangrove swamp where the poison men live, Spray answered.

The poison men? July and Liberty flashed.

Yes, we are sure that is where they hide, in the mangroves.

A tremor and a shadow passed through Liberty.

Spray felt her fear. *How far is Starfish Key? What would you say, Streak, in length? You know the kind the Navy used.*

Miles—oh, just eight or ten.

Eight or ten! both children exclaimed.

Don't worry, Streak and Spray immediately said, for they knew the children were thinking how long it would take them in the *Little Coconut.* *We'll take you on our backs and be there in a very short time.*

July did some quick distance-rate-time calculations and figured that if the dolphins cruised not even at full throttle, but say ten miles an hour, they would arrive at Starfish Key within an hour. It wouldn't be hard. They could do it all and get back to the houseboat in plenty of time.

All right, the twins agreed.

Ten miles an hour, forget it! July thought from Streak's back. These magnificent animals were going full throttle, close to eighteen miles an hour.

With Streak in the lead and Spray close behind, followed by eight other dolphins, all friends and relatives of the desperate Moon Spirit, the rescue team sliced across the moonlit waters of the Gulf. The twins felt themselves enveloped in a watery cocoon of silver light, speed, and wind. The images threaded their way through the childrens' and the dolphins' minds until they were all conjoined in one luminous web of thought and love for the beautiful white dolphin Moon Spirit.

20

Moon Spirit

THERE WAS A PORCELAIN FIGURINE on the twins' grand-ma's mantle back in Heart's Full, Kansas, that was said to have been made by a master Chinese potter. His formulas for glazes were the oldest and most difficult, having been handed down through centuries of masters and guarded with great secrecy. In the right hands, these formulas produced glazes of extraordinary delicacy. Pale and luminous, they surrounded a piece with a light of its own that was so subtle that the vase or bowl itself seemed to glow from within.

The image of their grandma's figurine in Kansas flashed in the twins' minds as they stood on the beach of Starfish Key and looked down at Moon Spirit, pale and luminous with a tinge of lavender.

Mother of pearl?

The lavender of an orchid's throat?

The images swirled between the twins. They heard a sudden ragged gasp.

Quick! Liberty flashed. *We can't just stand here!*

They remembered what Spray and Streak had said to do first—splash water onto her back and sides as soon as they got there. The message was now being sent with great urgency from all ten dolphins that swam anxiously just off the beach in the deeper water. July and Liberty began to run back and forth with handfuls of water. In a few trips, they had wet her down enough to notice a slight easing of her breathing.

Okay. Time for the big push, Liberty said. They both got down on their knees in the sand on one side of Moon Spirit and began to push. A dreadful feeling dropped like a boulder within their stomachs. She was immovable. There was no way two kids who only weighed seventy-nine pounds each could move this dolphin that weighed over five hundred pounds.

No way, no way! The thought was like cold lead in their minds. They tried a second push. Nothing.

Let's count . . . one . . . two . . . three, and on three, push together.

It did not work. Moon Spirit's breath had become ragged again. The twins felt panic well up inside them like bile. They wanted to gag, to throw up. They were both on the brink of tears. They felt Moon Spirit's life slipping out of her and were absolutely powerless to stop it. Their hearts raced. This was completely beyond them.

They looked up at the night sky. The stars hung like silver nuggets, cold and uncaring—who were they, after all, in this grand plan of a universe, but two insignificant specks on a beach with a dying dolphin from an ocean of a small planet in a minor galaxy? Did any of it make sense? Perhaps it was useless and silly to look for sense.

And then they felt the oddest sensation. It was as if their heads had suddenly become luminous, their skulls transparent and filled with a soft light that glinted with silver veins. The twins felt the power of the dolphins' voices offshore. They felt something grow within them. They felt their human edges dissolve, and yet their forms remained the same.

When it happened they did not count to three. They did not even take a deep breath. They only knew it was like sheet lightning in their brains. They felt Moon Spirit roll. Within seconds, they were standing in ankle-deep water supporting her. In those shallow inches of water, the dolphin immediately became light.

They were able to move her easily out into deeper water, but she was not well balanced. They kept their arms wrapped around her and walked deeper. Just as their feet left the ground, the other dolphins swam up and gently supported the children and Moon Spirit until all thirteen creatures swam as one under the dome of the starry night sky.

She was a battered soul, Moon Spirit. The children had swum with her and the other dolphins for a good fifteen minutes until the white dolphin regained her balance. Still they could tell that Moon Spirit was much different than the others. Her messages, if they could be called messages at all, were garbled. Within the web of images that connected the dolphins, those flowing from Moon Spirit hung lusterless and limp. Yet the ailing dolphin seemed to possess a deep tenderness, and frail as she was, a power of love and dearness that was as profound as it was extraordinary.

It was a stately procession. The children felt as if they were escorting a very ancient spirit from a long-ago world. Moon Spirit was weakened, perhaps, but nonetheless she remained a pale, luminous vessel for all that might be good in the world. And she was not a promise of goodness, but the very essence of it, for she was still in that sense complete, with all the colors of the spectrum, even though her body had been poisoned and tinged lavender.

21

Breakfast Table Blowout

LIBERTY, the dolphins told us they were sure those bad guys, the dumpers, were holed up in the mangrove swamp behind Starfish Key.

But how could they be? How could a mangrove swamp have a place where anybody could live except . . .

They had returned from their rescue mission long before sunrise, and now the family was just starting to stir on the deck below. The human day was beginning. Putnam Starbuck always began the day with a loud yawn and then elaborately blew his nose—a symphony of snorts, bellows, gasps, and sighs. He had allergies, and they seemed to gang up on him during the night. By the time he got through his first cup of coffee, he was fine. Amid these homey, familiar sounds emanating from downstairs, July felt Liberty's fear. He knew what it was . . .

Crocodiles!

Liberty, they are very rare. But he was familiar with

Liberty's deep aversion to reptiles of any sort. She barely tolerated the little twins' chameleons—Pinky, Madeline, Ken, and Barbie. No, Liberty was not reptile-inclined at all. She saw them as loathsome at best, and right now she saw herself as crocodile food.

She was remembering that strand of hair that had snagged on the witches' fingers so many months ago, trailing in the breeze over the dark, still waters of the swamp. A crocodile had probably picked up her scent. It was embedded deep within its primitive brain, a little chip in the ancient mainframe of the reptilian cerebellum. Primitive—ha! Primitive meant simple, in this case single-minded, with only one thought—meat— eat meat. Eat Liberty Bell Starbuck.

Shut up! J. B. teleblasted. *You're getting carried away, comparing these stupid animals to mainframe computers. Next you'll have them going to the Massachusetts Institute of Technology and winning Nobel prizes. Let me remind you, Liberty Bell Starbuck, that these crocs of the mangrove swamp are very rare, an endangered species, and harder to find than needles in a haystack. Here, it says it right in our nature guide to the Florida Keys.*

July swung out of his hammock and got a book from the shelf. He flipped it open and began to read, "The slender-snouted crocodile of these waters is very rare, secretive, and wary. It lurks near the tangled roots of the mangrove. It has red eyes, and . . ."

Liberty interrupted out loud. "Perfect pet for greedy toxic-waste dumpers."

"Oh, come off it, Liberty." July switched back into the telepathic channels. *We don't have a choice. It's like what Spray was saying—Moon Spirit is just part of it. Robbie is another part. All these things are part of the same problem—the problem Dad came to solve. We're all part of the web.*

She knew J. B. was right. Her dad had said it, too, when he had first told them about the turtles. "All the problems are related," he had said. The leatherbacks were not on the top of Put's priority list. "But," he had said, and the words came back to Liberty, "if we solve some of these other problems, we can't help but improve their lot as well."

Look, Liberty, we've already helped a little with the leatherbacks, and now we have a real chance to get at the source of it all, or at least a source of a lot of the trouble down here.

But where could they set up camp in a swamp of mangroves?

There are freshwater lakes totally enclosed by the mangroves, and there are islands within them. There are narrow beaches along the edges of the mangroves, too. It doesn't take much room to set up a shack, or a house on stilts, or a little cabin. They could even have a barge. It's not like they have to dig a foundation, you know.

"Aaah aaah aah choo!" Putnam had given his official blow-off-the-roof sneeze. The morning had begun.

The older twins could hear Charly and Molly begin to sniffle. They, too, had allergies. That was why their noses were always running. They sniffled a lot in the morning, especially if they hadn't had their allergy pills the evening before. According to Liberty, they were too lazy to use tissues. So everyone would hear them sniffling, or worse, see them wiping their snot-glazed noses on anything available—a handy forearm, a curtain, even their grandma's cat, Captain Fur, out in Heart's Full, Kansas, until she put a stop to it.

A few minutes later the Starbucks were all sitting at the breakfast table, except for Madeline, who was standing at the stove making pancakes.

Liberty sat directly across from Molly and Charly. They were a sight, she thought, from the far reaches of hell—their noses running, chameleons draped over every ear, with slender little triangular heads like frozen pendants. Liberty blinked and pictured crocodiles.

"Why are you wearing living jewelry to the breakfast table?"

They aren't crocodiles. We know what you were thinking. Charly and Molly telesynched the message. Telesynching was when both twins flashed exactly the same words at the same time.

And they aren't diamonds, either, Liberty flashed back.

Putnam, from behind his newspaper, sensed teletension in the air.

"It's their reward," he said.

"Reward?" July repeated, baffled. "Reward for what . . . being little sun-ripened pig droppings?"

"Don't start!" Madeline shook a spatula like a scolding finger at the children. "I have to fly back today. I want wonderful memories of my darling children."

Darling little pig droppings.

Darling bags of witches' warts.

You darling little swamp adders' bladders.

You son of a motherless goat.

You little mess of maggots.

You doo-doo heads.

When Charly and Molly got around to flashing "doo-doo heads," it was clear they were at the bottom of their word weaponry. Putnam, who had sensed the fight during the barrage of insulting names being tele-blasted across the breakfast table, had a glimmering that it was over now.

"They are being rewarded for having successfully trained four lizards, or rather chameleons, to drop from their ears like jewelry. It took patience, loving care, and tremendous imagination. We reward such virtues in our family. In this case, the reward is getting to wear Pinky, Ken, Barbie, and"—Putnam hesitated a bit and winced before saying the last name—"Madeline to the breakfast table for a brief period of time—at least until the pancakes get here."

"The breakfast table for living jewelry—yuck," July said. "Don't you think a dance would be more appropriate? You know, a prom or something."

"We're five years old, idiot!" Charly screamed at her brother. "Five year olds don't go to proms."

"Oooh!" said Molly, her blue eyes suddenly brighter

than cornflowers. "Maybe we should go to a prom. We could get in the Guinness Book of World Records."

"I like it, kids." Putnam beamed. "It's got style. World's Youngest Prom-goers."

"You'd have to wipe your noses to go to a prom. Even living jewelry cannot distract from those yucky dripping noses," Liberty said.

"Maybe," July offered, a glint in his eye, "you should consider a new training program for the lizards."

"What's that?" Charly and Molly asked.

"You could train them as a sanitation team—to lick up your noses."

"Oh, gross!" Madeline and Putnam said in unison.

"Truly disgusting," said Zanny, who had stayed out of the discussion thus far.

But from the look in Charly's and Molly's eyes, it was apparent that they did not find this notion disgusting or even outrageous.

Good grief, July, Liberty flashed. *You might have started something.*

Oh no! he telegroaned.

Madeline had just finished delivering the pancakes to the table and took a chair between July and Liberty. She patted Liberty's head affectionately. "Feels damp. You been swimming already this morning?"

"No. I mean, yes. You know, just a quick slide into the water." She laughed nervously. "Gets the sleep out of your eyes."

Charly and Molly slid their eyes toward J. B. They

saw him patting his own hair. Between J. B. and Liberty the channels clamped down immediately. Charly and Molly sensed this. They looked slyly at their older brother and sister. They were being shut out, left out.

There was nothing a five year old dreaded more from older brothers and sisters than being Not Included. The whole ethics system of five year olds hung on two-word phrases. "Left out," "too young," "not included." And their defense was a two word response, "Me, too!"

For a long time now, Molly and Charly had had a suspicion they were being left out of something big, really big. They didn't like that feeling at all. There was going to be trouble soon, and it would be coming from them, double barreled—or just plain double trouble.

22

Double Trouble Starts Up

JULY AND LIBERTY had decided to go to the mangrove swamp that night. They waited until their family was sound asleep. Even good old Bandit seemed asleep, with his long bill tucked into his feathers and his head more or less nestled into a wing, as he perched on the picket fence. A crescent moon was climbing high into the sky.

Liberty's eyes widened. The moon was sliding into the part of the skylight with the only piece of lavender glass. Then suddenly that moon was no longer a moon, but a dolphin riding through the night sky. Had Moon Spirit climbed to her moon at last? Liberty's heart raced. They must get to the mangrove swamp—soon!

We can go now, July flashed. He was amazed at how quickly Liberty was out of bed for someone who had real fears about going into the mangrove swamp.

They crawled out their window and slid down the slide. By now they were well practiced. They swam around to the *Little Coconut*. Liberty was first, and when she hauled herself over the edge of the boat, she gave a little gasp. There it was, waiting for them—double trouble sitting on the floorboards of the boat—Charly and Molly, complete with their Davy Crockett caps, and smiling, no less. Chameleons rested in scrolls on their bare shoulders.

Hi guys! they flashed and smiled more smugly.

Good grief, telesighed July, who had just climbed on board and taken in the situation. *Talk about Mission Impossible—this is it!*

Believe me, the Alamo was peanuts next to this.

There you go, teleblasted Molly. *You're making those snotty big-kid jokes that we don't understand.*

The Alamo was no joke, stupids, and neither is this.

We feel left out.

We know, replied Liberty. *You're always feeling left out, and you think it is the worst thing that can happen.*

Well, it is, said Charly.

No, it isn't. People can die, you know, get fatal illnesses. Children become orphans all the time—their parents get killed in car crashes, plane crashes—that's worse, you know.

Lighten up, July, Liberty said. The little twins' eyes had begun to brim with tears. They were thinking of their mother flying back to Washington that morning, and how she flew down almost every week to visit them. *We can't have them starting to cry and getting all slobbery out loud. It'll trigger their allergies, and they'll start sniffling, and we'll wake up everybody, or we'll drown in their snot.*

In other words, we're stuck with them.

Looks that way.

Relief swept across the little twins' faces.

This is dangerous business.

That's okay, they both said. To Charly and Molly the idea of danger was not nearly so scary or sad as that of becoming orphans.

Okay, you have to do exactly what Liberty and I say.

We will.

Promise?

I promise.

I promise.

Okay, put on your life jackets.

The mangrove swamp was just a few miles away, and with the favorable wind they would get there quickly. Of course, once there they could not sail through the narrow channels that were completely sheltered from the wind. They would not be able to use their engine, either, for they must move quietly and not be detected.

Their plan was relatively simple. They would steal into the mangroves and find out precisely if and where the toxic-waste criminals had set up their base. Hopefully, there would be plenty of incriminating evidence that would be a dead giveaway, or rather, a toxic giveaway, to their criminal activities.

Liberty and July had already stowed the Polaroid

flash camera kits their grandma had given them all for Christmas. And Charly and Molly, who had no idea of what this mission was really about, had seen them stow the cameras in the *Little Coconut* and figured out that this had something to do with the adventure. So they had brought theirs, too.

There was, then, ample technology for collecting evidence, if indeed there was any to collect. But July and Liberty had a hunch that there would be. It was hard to imagine that the dolphins, those quiet, watchful sentries of the ocean, would be wrong about something like this.

It was too bad the dolphins could not accompany the children into the mangrove swamp, but the water was not salty there. It turned brackish, and then sometimes it ran into freshwater lakes. It was shallow, too. In short, it was simply not good water in any sense for dolphins, so the children had to go alone.

The wind was on their stern quarter, pushing them gently through the Gulf waters with which they were now so familiar. Liberty and July had become good sailors. They handled the boat with ease and precision. Because they could sense the slightest variation in wind direction on the backs of their necks, or even earlobes, they no longer needed to look at the telltale strings of yarn that flew off the halyards, indicating wind direction. They could expertly trim the sails to the shape and force of the wind to get the most power.

The *Little Coconut*, although bulky and no clipper

ship, slid through the water with grace and ease. There were no lines dragging, and in her sails, no luff—those wrinkles where the wind spills from the canvas and goes unused. They passed a familiar sandbar, which on this night was presided over by a single great white heron that stood like a white slash in the night.

Soon Starfish Key was drawing up abeam of them. Had it been just last night that they had rescued Moon Spirit and swam with her into deeper water? It seemed years ago. Liberty looked up at the sky. A dolphin moon it was—leaping toward a star, now luminous and white, no tinge of lavender.

July let out on the sail, and Liberty, who was at the helm, or tiller, steered the *Little Coconut* a point or two off the wind. They would drop down behind Starfish Key now, to the bad water side. They warned Charly and Molly to keep their hands in the boat and not to touch anything.

The wind died suddenly. They decided to wait a few minutes in the hope that it would come back up. They did not want to have to turn on the engine. But there was a fetid, close smell in the air, and all the children noticed that the currents swirling around them carried a lot of garbage—plastic containers, nylon fishing nets, small buoys adrift from the crab or lobster pots they had once marked.

Look at that! flashed Molly. She was pointing at a bright, fluorescent-orange pot buoy. It was trailing seaweed and some plastic line. Ensnared in the mess of weed and line was a dead starfish. But what a strange starfish it was.

Don't touch! Liberty and July both flashed, for they were drifting down upon it. Their eyes widened, and they felt a queasiness in their stomachs as they counted the arms of the starfish.

One . . . two . . .

Three . . . four . . .

Five . . . six . . .

Oh no, seven!

How weird!

And look, July, they're all twisted and misshapen.

They look like corkscrew macaroni, Molly flashed.

And cheese, Charly added.

Oh yuck, Liberty and July telesynched.

I think we've entered the weirdness zone.

The smell had grown heavier in the air. The sand-bars seemed empty of the usual bird life, and the currents and eddies swirled with the trash of so-called higher life forms—their beer cans, their plastic detergent bottles, a rubber thong—the relics of what the world liked to call civilization. This was the weirdness zone.

But it was not called that on the chart. Liberty, like all good sailors who sail at night or in precarious waters, held the tiller in one hand and a chart in the other. Molly held a flashlight for her. Liberty looked down at the pool of light on the chart. Where they were was labeled Hawk Eye Channel. It ran behind

Starfish Key and slipped into a wide pool called Palmetto Lagoon. Once in the lagoon they must be very vigilant, for it shoaled up drastically, even for a shallow draft boat like the *Little Coconut*.

July and Charly would be minding the daggerboard. The daggerboard, or centerboard, was a piece of wood that hung down through the center of the boat directly into the water, like a fin. Unlike a keel, which was fixed, a daggerboard could be raised and lowered by pulling on a line. So if the daggerboard touched bottom, it could quickly be raised, and there would still be water under the boat before they ran aground.

Every time they had gone to Lonely Key they had pulled up their daggerboard before surfing into the beach. They knew they'd have no trouble now, however, if they followed the markers, for within Palmetto Lagoon there was a deeper channel. But this channel was very narrow and only a few feet wide, and they knew they had to be careful to stay within it.

Liberty spotted the buoy marking the beginning of the channel, called the Ditch Line.

Is the compass out and lit? Liberty flashed to July.

Yep.

Okay, the course is 180 degrees south.

Correct.

Putnam had given the children a compass as a present, along with a set of parallel rules. He had then taught them some basic navigation skills in plotting a course. This was something at which July had become especially good.

To figure out the course to the mangrove swamp, July had taken the chart, which had a compass rose printed in a lower corner. The compass rose was on every official marine navigational chart. It was two circles, one printed within the other. The outer circle, or ring, indicated the true direction, or the geographic location, of the North Pole. The inside ring showed the magnetic North Pole, where the compass needle points.

Navigators always plot courses according to the inner circle, the magnetic direction. July was using the parallel rules, two transparent rulers that were hinged together by crosspieces, so that one slid above the other, always parallel. He had laid them on the chart along the Ditch Line that cut across Palmetto Lagoon.

He drew a line on the chart from the point at which they would enter the mangrove swamp, at the beginning of the Ditch Line, to its end. He then stepped the rules toward the compass rose in the lower corner, being careful to keep them at the same angle to the sea line, which was the route along the Ditch to the mangrove swamp.

When the transparent rules were over the compass rose, July read the inside circle for the magnetic direction, which was 180 degrees south. If they stayed exactly within four degrees of this number, they would be fine and not run aground. Liberty had to steer a very precise course. It was like tightrope walking. Charly would shine the light on the compass. July would teleflash the compass readings.

They had begun sailing along the Ditch Line in a light breeze.

Okay, you're doing good, doing good, 180 south southwest. There was a pause of nearly half a minute, then July flashed, *182, Liberty, south southwest . . . overcorrection, 179 south southeast. Bring her up a bit.* So they sailed for the better part of an hour.

The Ditch Line ended in a narrow neck of water that led into the mangrove swamp. They lowered the sail now. From this point on they would have to proceed by pushing the boat with a pole from the stern. July took over the poling. Liberty swallowed hard and held the edges of the chart more tightly between her fingers. The chart, of course, was useless within the tangled channels of the swamp. They had entered a region that was virtually chartless in its twisted, ever-shifting intricacies.

I think I can, I think I can. The words of the old children's book came back to her, about the little engine that could go up the steep hill with the heavy load. The load of fear Liberty carried now seemed every bit as heavy. And her brother and little sisters felt her fear, too. Perhaps not as strongly, but they felt it nonetheless.

Liberty, July flashed, *let's try to be rational.*

I'm trying.

Remember, this is not really the same mangrove swamp we first came through that day when Dad mentioned the crocodile, and yes, where your hair got snagged.

But it's connected to that one. Crocodiles can travel. Don't you know they have a range of twenty miles or something?

I don't think they'd come that far for you, Charly flashed.

Thanks!

But oddly enough, Liberty did feel a little bit better. Sometimes an insult helped one rally even quicker than logic.

It might not have been the same mangrove swamp, but it felt identical, the same dark maze of narrowing channels, the tangled branches reaching from overhead like snaggly witches' fingers. At night, of course, it was even worse. There was no blue sky beyond the branches, only a sinister embroidery of black against black.

Was it just the darkness that made it feel that way, or did the branches seem to be lower? Was the arch of witches' fingers pressing down? Liberty hunched her shoulders and tried to shrink herself as small as Charly and Molly. In the dark she could see the glowing yellow slits of the chameleons' eyes, as the small reptiles scampered around on the little twins' shoulders. She tried very hard not to think of the chameleons as junior crocodiles—mini-crocs. She felt a convulsion of nervous laughter rise in her telepathic channels. There was a flash from her brother and sisters.

Calm down!

You're getting giddy! July's message twinkled in her brain.

And then not five seconds later, on her neck, the back of her neck, a finger scratched, snaring a piece of her hair.

Charly and Molly lurched at her, slamming their hands over her mouth. July nearly dropped the pole, for the telescream had cracked like lightning in all of their heads.

It was just a branch. I'm okay. Let me breathe, Liberty flashed.

Get in the bottom of the boat, J. B. flashed back. *The branches are really low here. Get up there where Charly is. You can put the sail bags over you, or even the sails, for that matter.*

It was a good idea. Under the clean, salt-sprayed material of the sails, Liberty felt better. The tangled darkness and still black waters of the swamp seemed to recede. It was as if she had been instantly transported to a cleaner, lighter, fresh world of crisp sea breezes and cresting blue waves. She could conjure up the whispers of long-forgotten winds they had sailed close hauled to, or reached across, or run straight down. She could see the silver arcs flying against the bright blue clearness of the Florida sky. Her heart stopped racing, and she felt a warm little hand seek out her own. Charly had crept under the sail with her.

I like sailing with you this way, Charly telewhispered. *You make me feel the breezes and remember the dolphins. Do you think we'll ever get to meet them?*

Maybe.

Do you think they'll like us the way they liked you?

Sure.

Do you think they'll let us ride with them, too?

Liberty and July had told the little twins all about the dolphins, and how it was because of them that they had really begun this mission.

Probably. Don't see why not.

I think you're very brave, Liberty, Charly flashed with great solemnity.

Oh, come on! If I were brave I wouldn't be hiding under a sail from a crocodile who probably doesn't know I exist.

But if you're not scared, there is nothing to be brave about. It's no big deal. Remember what Dad always says.

What?

You know, that thing in Latin.

Oh, Apparere Es Eres.

Yeah. Half of life is showing up.

I wonder if it counts if you do it under a sail and sail bag?

Sure it does. You're here, aren't you?

But in a bag, so to speak.

Yeah, but look, you make the blackness disappear, you make the darkness light, and fill my head with blue sky, and make me smell the salt and feel wind pictures in my brain.

Maybe you have holes in your head. A chuckle shimmered between them in the telepathic channels, and Charly squeezed her big sister's hand.

Tell me about the lavender dolphin again, the one called Moon Spirit.

Well, once upon a real time, like the day before yesterday . . .

23

Caught!

LIBERTY HAD JUST GOTTEN to the part where Streak had told them about Moon Spirit's fantastic leaps beyond Cobb's Reef. She and Charly were both trying to imagine the great sprays and towers of splashing white water, when a scratchy voice rasped out of the night.

"Get out! Get out! Turn around!"

It's Robbie! July flashed. *I don't believe it! It's him!*

Liberty stuck her head out from under the sail bag and peeked over the gunwales. The alleyway of water had bulged into a larger, round pool. In the center was a small island, and on the thin strip of beach crouched Robbie. She could not see his face clearly, but she knew as surely as she knew her own name that his eyes were at last wide open, but in terror.

"Quick! Get out before it's too late!" he cried.

And then everything seemed to happen at once. Liberty felt a fierce tug on her arm, pulling her back down. She heard a crash of something falling from above. There was the clatter of the pole against the gunwales, and July and Molly screamed out loud. There was static in the telepathic channels, then a blackout.

The *Little Coconut* stopped dead in its tracks. Bumps, thumps, and gasps could be heard coming from Molly and July, but beneath the sail bag Charly and Liberty were stiff, stiff as the chameleons now frozen in terror on Charly's shoulder, stiff with fear.

Stay still. The two words flickered dimly in her brain. The channels were opening up slightly, with the first glimmerings of a message from July.

"Okay. We got them rascals!"

"Holy cow! It's two more brats. What are we running here, a nursery school?"

"Well, would you prefer the Feds?"

Liberty, Charly, stay under cover. They think there are only two of us. Just freeze. The channels were wide open once more. Molly could be heard whimpering aloud as well as telepathically, and she was in no shape to send any other kind of message. And Charly, as molecularly identical as any twin ever was to another, was receiving a super-intense dose of fear. If one were to compare it to sound recording, the fear Charly was experiencing would be stereo of the highest fidelity. She was awash with her mirror-image identical twin's whimpers and terror.

Liberty was gradually collecting her wits. *Try not*

*to tremble, Charly. The sail bag must not move. They
don't think we're here. They don't know about us . . .
yet.* Then, switching over to July's frequency, she
flashed, *What exactly is happening?*

*They got some kind of big net thing around us. It's
around the whole back half of the boat. But it's caught over
the daggerboard, so it's not covering the bow . . .* There
was a pause in the flashing. *Okay, now don't panic, but
I think they are tightening this net around us, and they are
going to lift us off the boat. I have to help Molly here. She's
a mess.* July switched entirely into Molly's channel.

Thank goodness, Liberty thought, that since London they had become more skillful at moving completely into their little sisters' telepathic channels. And
now, if indeed they were taking July and Molly off the
boat, this would be a true test of remote teleflashing:
to see if they could all teleflash from greater distances,
and not have to be under the same roof.

A harsh voice shot out of the night. "Stay where
you are, kid. Don't move."

Good grief! He's carrying a gun! July exclaimed.

"We're going to truss you kids up tight as turkeys
in this here net, and git you off this boat. Got the
rope, Cuda?"

Cuda!

The name seemed to glower in the still night air.
Liberty remembered the man from the night they had
first seen the *Shark Bite*, and then again in Key West—
tall and bony, the skin that seemed too thin and fit

too tightly, making him look like a walking skeleton. Mostly, however, she remembered the pale, thin lips that stretched over his pointed teeth and gave him the look of a barracuda.

Molly and Charly's channels were now fully opened as well. Molly, still whimpering, was sending a message to Charly.

It's just like Roly Poly Pudding.

Charly cringed, and static crackled in the channels between the little twins.

Charly and Molly's favorite story to hate was *Roly Poly Pudding*. They dared themselves to look at the dreadful picture of Tom Kitten being rolled up into a piece of dough and tied with string to bake in an oven.

That's what they're doing to me. Wrapping me up in a bundle. I'm a sausage! Molly telewhimpered. *They're going to bake me!*

Maybe you won't taste good! Charly flashed the voice of Samuel Whiskers, the villain. *"You wouldn't be a good pudding."*

The little twins could not help themselves. Their scary thoughts about *Roly Poly Pudding* were like a runaway freight train in their telepathic channels. The old illustrations from the book flickered brightly in their brains.

Liberty felt the boat rock in the water and tip to one side.

We're going, July flashed.

Oh no. Liberty felt something die within her.

Then sharply, like a beam of bright light, like a laser cutting through her despair, *Keep the channels open, Liberty. We must stay in touch. We can't lose touch.* July flashed the stern warning. This would be the ultimate driveway test of their long distance telepathic abilities.

"There are getting to be too many of these kids now," the rough voice was saying. "We're going to have to keep them tied up, under lock and key."

"They ain't goin' no place." It was a thin, flat, raspy voice. Liberty was sure it belonged to Cuda. "Not with Old Croc cruising around."

Oh no! Liberty felt a blackness well up in her stomach. Charly clasped her hand more tightly.

Okay, July teleflashed. *They are setting us down on the ground. Unless they roll us . . .*

Don't say roll, July, Molly whimpered. *It reminds me of you-know-what.*

Well, I don't know how they'll get us farther without untying us and letting us out of this net bag. July was intent on giving a play-by-play description in order to keep the channels open.

I don't know what I should do, July. We're still here on the boat. If I can get away, I guess I should sail for home and get help as fast as I can. But I'm not sure I can get away without them finding out. Oh, this is a mess.

Don't panic. We have to wait and see what happens, what they do with us, then make a plan.

"Well, Cuda, to be on the safe side we got to keep

them in the shack. We can shut them up in that back room."

"Maybe you're right. This ain't like dealing with one kid. This is triple . . ."

And when Cuda said the word "triple," something began to glimmer in Liberty's brain.

Triple my foot. This is double, double trouble squared again!

I think you've got something, Liberty. July's response came twinkling through the channels.

Yeah, let me think about this, let me think about it. Don't panic. It now was Liberty who was flashing the "be calm" warnings to July. *I just need a little time here. We're not twins for nothing. Double the danger, double the fun, double the trouble, and double the power.*

24

The Power of Twins

"IT WOULD HAVE BEEN a heck of a lot better if we'd caught ourselves some floaters with that darned net, instead of these little kids."

"Sculp, you don't know that. Them floaters that come in here, they don't talk no English, just Spanish. How we going to tell them how to put the stuff down? It would be just like that white dolphin."

Moon Spirit!

Liberty's and Charly's eyes widened. They were crouched outside the shack where the three men had taken July and Molly, and they were peering in through a window. After locking July, Molly, and Robbie in a back room, the men had settled down at a table and were pouring drinks from a bottle of whiskey.

"Cuda's right. You can't train them floaters to do anything. Be just like the dolphin," said the third man, a fat man they called Ghee.

"But them kids ain't dumb," Sculp was saying.

"They're going to know what that stuff is, that it ain't no candy they're diving down with."

"Yeah, well it's always a trade off. You think we're going to be able to train a bunch of them dumb floaters who don't speak no English how to use that scuba gear before the next shipment comes in?"

Oh no! Liberty tele-exclaimed.

What?

Liberty didn't even want to tell Charly, but the picture came together clearly, and the images were too bright to prevent Charly from perceiving them. The creeps had been waiting for Cuban and Haitian refugees. That was the reason for the net rigged in the mangroves.

They want to strap that poison stuff to Molly and July and Robbie, and make them dive down and dump it? Why can't they just throw it overboard? Will it float or something? Why do they have to use children?

Why did they use Moon Spirit? Liberty asked, as she saw all the dreadful pieces of the dark puzzle fall into place. *Did they use Robbie, too?*

No, July flashed back. *They haven't used Robbie—yet.* The driveway experiment was working. The channels were open and functioning, though they were definitely not under the same roof.

But then how did Robbie get those purple hands? Was he kidnapped before?

No, no. He told me the whole story, Liberty, and it's awful. Robbie was just playing where he shouldn't have been. He took that little skiff of Bert's to a key near Starfish and ran into these guys. They flung some of the poison stuff at him while they were trying to run him off. Then they got nervous that his hands would give everything away, so they've been out looking for him ever since.

But Liberty, get back on track, July continued. *I know it's terrible what they're planning for us, but get back to thinking about, you know, double trouble.*

Yeah, you're right, July. I'm just so shocked. This is so . . .

But July deflected her thoughts. *Tell me, what are they doing right now? I can't see them.*

Well, they're just drinking whiskey.

Good. Maybe they'll get drunk.

That might be helpful, Liberty replied, considering the possibilities.

Now what happens when people get drunk? she thought.

The men were continuing to talk. "That stuff ain't so bad if it just gets on you like the kid got it on his hands—just burns you. Don't mess up your insides. That's what the guy from New York said."

Oh great, flashed Liberty. *It just burns our hands into purple corduroy.*

It was the fat man who was talking, the one called Ghee. "That guy said if it hits you in open air you just get burned, but if it hits you in an ox . . . hup . . ." Three times he tried to say the phrase, and on the fourth he got it fairly straight. "An oxygen-deprived environment." He spoke the words slowly, with all the concentration of a tightrope walker stepping across a high wire. "Like for instance," only the words came out "frinzdance," and he hiccuped again. "Frinzdance water, well, then you got problems, cause it goes into a capillary action, and . . ."

"Sakes, Ghee, you sure are smart."

"He ain't that smart. Just got a bunch of fancy words," Cuda said. Liberty shuddered. There was something about Cuda's voice and the way he spoke that made the words drip like slow, thick poison off his thin lips. "What he means is that it messes up your brain if you contact it direct underwater. And that last canister we sent old Whitey down with must have had a leak. Can't 'rust those New York people."

It was growing more horrible by the second. So this explained Moon Spirit's tragic condition. Liberty could only hope that Robbie had not yet been sent on an underwater mission. Purple corduroy hands, compared to permanent brain damage, now seemed a mere scratch. The poison must have saturated Moon Spirit's system.

Liberty! Liberty! July was practically shouting her name in the channels. *Get back on the track.*

What?

Cuda's gettin' drunk! Didn't you catch that—"Can't 'rust those New York people."

Oh, I guess I was thinking rusty cans or something.

No. He's starting to mush up his words. Listen!

"All them . . ." There was a pause while Cuda swallowed a burp. The slow poison of his voice started to drip again, but July was right. He was slurring his words. "New York guysh are the shame . . . cheap . . . dey don't shink nothing about us doing all the risky work."

"God bless you, Cuda, you sshpeak de truth." Sculp had begun to slobber in his glass.

See! J. B. flashed.

Yes, I certainly am beginning to see. Liberty saw what alcohol was doing to the men's brains, wrecking their speech. They slurred their words. Extra letters doubled up in the wrong places, stretching out words like thick globs of pulled taffy. And of course, when a person was drunk there could be vision problems, too.

Where you think there is one image, there might be two. The thought crept through the channels in a slow twinkling from July.

Double, double . . . Liberty's mind was working with the doubleness of it all. *Double vision, double trouble . . . I got it!* Liberty exclaimed, and the channels between all four twins became brilliant with the flash of her inspiration.

Then it was as if the three men were playing right into her hands.

"I wonder what exactly it doesh to your brain?" Sculp was saying.

"Oh, probably messesh with your eyes, makesh you have double vision . . ."

Holy double mackerel! all four twins telesynched.

We're in like Flynn, Liberty.

Don't count our chickens before they hatch, Jelly Bean.

Don't count your Starbucks before they hatch! replied J. B.

Okay. Liberty's hair had been pulled back in a pony tail. She tucked the tail into the rubber band and pulled out some wisps in front of her ears. She now looked just like her twin brother. She flashed the beginning of the strategy again.

Remember folks, we start slow. I'll take Cuda, and Charly is going to take Ghee. Ghee seems very suggestible. Then Charly will switch to Cuda, and I'll begin work on Sculp. We'll just sort of rotate.

Luckily, the men were seated in positions where they each had a view of a window. Liberty was going to begin with Cuda, but then he got up to get another bottle of whiskey.

So take it away, Charly!

Charly climbed atop an old crate near the window where she was posted, and poked her head up. Ghee was gazing directly at the window at just that moment, recalling his dear old Mom in his alcoholic daze. Charly smiled sweetly at Ghee. He blinked, looked into his glass, studied the contents, and then looked up again. No Charly.

Great timing, Charly. We mustn't overdo it. Give him a rest. Let him think it was all in his head.

It was Liberty's turn now. She slowly rose up in

the window, then sank down. Not too fast, not too slow. She remained visible about as long as a first-grade teacher holds up a flash card. Cuda scowled at the living flash card. That was all. He was going to be a tough customer, Liberty thought, but she'd get to him.

Several minutes had elapsed before Ghee looked out the window again. He was sure things had returned to normal, but still he slid his eyes up slowly from his glass of whiskey. Charly tried an Aunt Honey smile this time—lots of teeth. Then, as an added touch, crossed her eyes. Ghee jerked in his chair as if an electrical current had gone through him.

"What the heck's wrong with you?" Cuda growled.

"Nothin', Cuda, nothing."

Change in strategy, Liberty flashed. *I think the time might be right to begin work on Sculp. I'll get back to Cuda later.* She crept around to the window opposite Sculp. He was even more responsive than she had hoped.

"What'd you say happens to your brain with that stuff, Cuda?"

Quick, Charly, get to Cuda's window, Liberty flashed.

Charly popped up just as Cuda was raising his eyes to the window, hoping not to see Liberty. But instead there was the little red-haired one with a lizard plastered on each shoulder. Cuda jumped up from the table, and his chair fell over behind him with a clatter.

"Where them kids?" He raced to the door of the

room where Robbie, Molly, and July were, unbolted it, and flung it open.

"Did you see it? Did you see it, too, Sculp?" Ghee was slobbering.

"No . . . no . . . no," Sculp protested. In his mind he was not seeing the faces in the window, but a pile of scrambled eggs and the somber words from an ad he had seen on television. "This is your brain; this is your brain on drugs. . . ." "No, no," he rasped.

When Cuda flung open the door, he saw all three children in a corner, looking appropriately scared. Anything that cowered in his presence made Cuda relax. He shut the door, returned to the table, poured himself another drink, and cursed himself for being so silly. He gave a little shrug and looked out the window at the same time Ghee did. Right on cue, Charly and Liberty sprang up.

Sculp, who had been on the brink of hysteria, crossed over. "I saw 'em, too!" he screamed. Ghee and Cuda raced for the door, stumbling on top of each other. But when they finally got outside, there was no sign of anything.

The confusion gave a camouflage of noise. Quick as a wink, July, Robbie, and Molly formed a human pyramid with Molly at the top. She was careful to cover her eyes and face with one hand, the way July told her. With her other hand she smashed a number ten can of peeled tomatoes through the window. The glass shattered. She knocked out the smaller, loose pieces that might cut them. Then she crawled out, and Robbie and July followed. Freedom! The very thought bloomed like an exotic night plant, rare and beautiful—but they wasted no time.

Phase Two of the strategy had commenced, and the three men were playing right into the children's hands.

"It's our brains. I just know it, it's our brains," Sculp was saying desperately.

"He's right, Cuda!" Ghee blubbered. "We probably had an exposure to that diploiii . . ." He could hardly get the words out.

"But we weren't in an oxygen-free environment."

"But but bu . . . we were in a worse one."

"What's that, Ghee?"

"Alcohol . . . alcohol and that diploi-stuff don't mix. It's prrrobably a catalyst . . ."

"A what?"

"Alcohol slows oxygen to your brain and catalyzes with diploiii—" Oh yes, Ghee's dear old Mom had wanted him to be a scientist. He should have been a scientist, but no, instead he was stuck in a swamp with these dummies who dumped poison and drank.

"Shut up!" snarled Cuda.

But just at that moment, from behind a twisted tree with broad, heavy leaves, two identical faces peeped . . .

. . . and then two more from behind another tree. It was bedlam. Identical faces were popping out of everywhere, and the three men were staggering about, bleary with alcohol, their heads laced with double images and nightmares about their own dying brains. Sculp was muttering, ". . . this is your brain before diploidmishamacallit; this is your brain after . . ."

Robbie had to run faster than any of them, for he was determined that Sculp, Cuda, and Ghee would think that he, too, was a double image. Although he could not comprehend the silent signals crackling through the channels between the twins, he realized that they had a special way of communicating, and he half understood what they were doing. July had already told him the general strategy when they had been shut in the room.

The twins were leading the three men around in a series of tangled circles, but each loop of each circle brought them closer to where the *Little Coconut* was tied up. Their strategy was to get in the boat and slide away into the night of the swamp.

It would be hard finding their way out of the maze, but July learned from talking to Robbie in the shack that he had some sense of the geography of the swamp. All they had to do was get out into the more open waters of the lagoon. They would have to resist turning on their engine until then, for any noise would be a dead giveaway as to where they were, leaving a sound-trail clear as a bell for Cuda and company to follow.

We're almost there! Liberty flashed.

One more loop to mix them up, and then into the boat, all of us! July flashed.

"Where are those gol' darn brats?"

"What they doing to us? How many are there?"

The children had made it to the boat. July lifted the pole to push them silently into the dark waters. They huddled low. July even tried to crouch as he poled. Then suddenly, Molly realized that the communications coming through so strong and clear were not from the little figure balled up beside her. That ball was slightly bigger than it should be.

The twins had been so used to being a foursome, and had become so adept at communicating telepathically even when out of visual range, that they hadn't noticed the actual physical absence of one. There were, after all, four people in the boat, but one was Robbie, and the unmistakable and terrible realization flashed between all the channels.

Charly's missing! She's left behind!

What do you mean missing? I'm just taking one more loop. I'm really mixing these guys up.

Then there was a terrible scream. Charly felt a bony hand grab her with incredible strength. The long fingers encircled her entire shoulder joint. Another arm grabbed her around her rib cage. She felt her feet leaving the ground . . . she was caught. The other three twins and Robbie froze in the bottom of the *Little Coconut*.

25

Quicksilver
With Purple Hands

WE CAN'T leave without her! Molly was flashing frantically.

Don't worry. We won't. I just can't believe it. It was all going so well!

Charly, Charly, what's he doing to you?

He's holding me upside down over his head. Oh dear, I think Ken just ran down his shirt. He's wiggling around a lot.

Charly, are you wearing your press-on nails?

Of course. Don't be silly.

July and Liberty were amazed as they tuned into the channels between the little twins. Charly and Molly seemed relatively calm. They were communicating fairly clearly.

Well, use them! Molly shrieked the command through the channels.

Oh my gosh! Charly exclaimed. Their parents and Zanny were always warning them about poking eyes out with their press-on nails. She guessed the time had come. Could she really do it?

Of course you can! flashed Molly.

You don't know how hard it is. I'm hanging upside down over this dope's head, and he's not walking very steady. He's still drunk.

Good!

But I might not hit the target.

Try!

Cuda had been holding Charly up over his head, but now he rested her directly on top and clamped her down. This position held her more firmly and gave her less freedom of movement, but she was at least face forward and could look down the front of Cuda. Charly imagined she looked like some sort of crazy hat—a living hat to match the living jewelry that was running around inside Cuda's shirt, for now both Ken and Barbie were making tracks all over his bony body. He removed one hand as he reached inside his shirt to get the chameleons.

I see his belly button.

Is he an innie or an outtie?

Outtie.

Hit it!

The living hat known as Charly slid a bit. Perfect angle. The little dagger nails shot out. Bull's eye!

There was a grunt. Charly felt Cuda crumple. She blasted off him and raced into the swamp. The water was over her head, but she didn't care. She was swimming for all she was worth.

This way! This way! all three twins flashed. They had seen her dash into the swamp. Charly turned and began swimming toward them. And then something terrible happened. A bellow shook the entire swamp, and from a bank they heard a scuttling sound and branches breaking. Red-rimmed eyes glared like torches in the swamp night.

"It's Croc!" Liberty screamed, and this time she screamed out loud. The immense reptile was swimming directly for Charly.

No more living hat, thought Charly. I'm going to be dead—very soon. Dead meat, dead hat, what's the difference? And I'm too scared to even cry. Charly curled into a little ball and began to sink to the bottom of the murky water of the swamp.

She waited for the sound of snapping jaws, the first tearing pains as her flesh was ripped from her bones. She hoped he would not eat her head first. She wanted to be dead by the time the crocodile snapped her neck. She pressed her lips together harder, but she knew she could not hold her breath a second longer. There was a terrible crushing feeling in her chest. She was running out of air, but how long did she have to wait to be eaten?

Charly burst through the surface of the water, gasping for air. It was like the Fourth of July. Fireworks seemed to be exploding everywhere in the night of the swamp. Flashes of light illuminated the *Little Coconut*, which tipped to one side at an alarming angle. And then Charly realized what was happening. July, Liberty, Molly, and Robbie were leaning over the side, madly taking flash pictures of Old Croc.

They think this is fun! They want pictures of me being eaten alive. Oh boy, this takes the cake! Charly was furious.

Then Molly flashed—not a bulb but a thought— *Swim for the boat, you dope. I'm down to my last bulb.*

Oh, Jeez Louise! Charly suddenly realized this was her chance. The crocodile was being blinded by the blasting lights of the flashbulbs. It was totally transfixed and confused. Charly swam like crazy for the boat. She clambered onto a gunwale, and Robbie and July quickly pulled her on board.

Start the engine, Liberty! July flashed, although there was hardly a need for silence now. Their cover was certainly blown.

Liberty started the engine. Meanwhile, July reloaded the camera.

"We're okay now." Liberty was speaking aloud. "Charly is here, safe and sound. I can't believe how smart you were, Charly, to sink like that. Remember on 'Wild World of Animals'? They said that if a crocodile is coming for you and you can't reach shore, the best thing is to sink down and pretend you're part of the scenery—that way you're much less threatening. July, what are you doing?" Liberty asked.

"Just a few shots for old time's sake."

Cuda, Sculp, and Ghee were standing on the beach—or rather, Ghee had fallen into a drunken stupor. They had come down for the entertainment of seeing a child devoured by a crocodile.

"Smile, guys!" July shouted, as he snapped their picture.

"What if they follow us?" Charly asked, still trembling.

"They won't," Robbie said, smiling broadly. He held up a key ring in his purple hand. "I swiped their boat keys."

"When?" asked Liberty.

"On one of our loops when we were still close to the shack. I'm quick, you know." Robbie snapped his purple fingers in the air.

Liberty remembered how Robbie had gotten the soda out of the refrigerator case at the Grubby Duck that day, and flipped the money to Ally, and how Ally had said he could eat a snow cone with his feet. He was quick all right. Using Charly's flash camera, he had shot more pictures and reloaded the camera quicker than anyone. He was quicksilver with purple hands.

26

A Saint Named Bandit

VALTERO SANCHEZ scanned the dark water. His eyes were old and dim, but even so they had become accustomed to the familiar shapes that might bob out of the night waters of the Gulf, indicating a *barquero*, a boat person.

The boat could be almost anything—a raft, a nest of inner tubes tied together, even a single inner tube. If the people had enough money before they left Cuba or Haiti, they might have even gotten hold of a small rowboat or skiff to rig a sail for the favorable southeasterly trade winds that blew toward the coast of Florida. If they were very lucky, they ran into Valtero, or people like him, before the lack of water made them go crazy and drink saltwater, or before sharks tore the last shreds of their sinking rafts out from under them.

Valtero would load these refugees into his boat, give them water, food, ointment for their parched and bleeding lips, and sail them to safety. But tonight there was no one—*nada*, nothing. No lumps melted out of the night, no shape to call out to, *"Hola, amigos! Estoy aqui para recibirlos. Cálmense, cálmense! Ustedes han llegado a los Estados Unidos."*

And always there was that terrible feeling as he called out into the night, the fear that when he shouted *"Amigos,"* there would be no answer. His breath would lock in his throat as he approached the silently floating raft, his ears straining for a gasp, a sigh, the weak cry of a baby. Too often the boat had been empty, the *barqueros* having died and slid into the sea. And too often he had found rafts floating with lifeless bodies. He tried, he tried so hard to get there in time, but an old man could only go so far in a small boat with a fifteen-horsepower engine.

Suddenly something caught his attention. It was no lump on the water, but a stirring of the still air overhead.

"Hola, Bandido! Dónde estabas? Qúe quieres, tu ave loca? Te has encontrado con algunos barqueros, ya?"

But it wasn't refugees Bandit had found. It was a pod of dolphins, his friends, clicking their distress and unable to help the children, who were beyond reach in the shallow, brackish waters of the swamp.

Valtero could tell there must be something wrong in the mangroves. Somehow, the one-eyed bird knew there was trouble. And indeed, a few hours earlier, Valtero had passed a group of dolphins that had been behaving oddly. They had come up to his boat; as usual, he had thrown them some live bait, but they had not seemed interested. They hadn't played off his bow waves or shown off with their fantastic leaps in the moonlight. They had been subdued. Why?

As he watched Bandit swoop low over the dolphins now in front of his boat, a sudden, terrible realization began to creep over him. Something was very wrong. Could the dolphins be warning Bandit? The trouble must be in a place where dolphins could not swim, but where birds could fly—in a place too shallow, or too poison!

Valtero's eyes opened in horror as he peered into the benign faces of the graceful mammals cruising slowly around his boat. Overhead, Bandit flew a straight, swift path. It was as if the bird had Valtero on a line and was reeling him in, toward an urgent destination. Valtero threw open the throttle of his boat and sped across the lagoon.

Fifteen minutes later, he arrived at the end of the Ditch Line just as the twins roared out of the swamp. Never had they been so glad to see anybody. On his small CB radio he immediately called the Coast Guard and the police. In no time, helicopters were swarming overhead as thick as mosquitoes at dusk. Coast Guard cutters appeared on the horizon, and one carried Putnam Starbuck and Zanny, looking stunned and frightened.

27

Double Relief

"INCONTROVERTIBLE EVIDENCE," the police officer was saying. "Detective Malone, I'd say the case against these guys is solid as anything."

"I'd say these kids have done my job for me. If this doesn't hold up in court, I don't know what will." The detective was studying a photograph. Although Croc was in the foreground of the picture, in the background were drums and cartons—some even labeled TOXIC WASTE. And on the thin strip of shore stood Cuda and Sculp, with Ghee in a crumpled heap at their feet.

"Well, how in the world did you children ever think of the bit with the flashbulbs?" Putnam sat in the police boat with Charly wrapped in a towel on his knees. Charly had long ago quit trembling, but Putnam, as he looked at the pictures of the crocodile in the water and the small blur that was his daughter swimming, began shaking violently. Zanny cuddled Molly.

"Well, Dad, it's straight out of your favorite movie," July said.

"Remember, *Rear Window?*" Liberty said.

"*Rear Window*, of course!" Putnam smiled.

"Of course!" exclaimed Zanny, for she too knew the old movie. Jimmy Stewart was in a wheelchair with a broken leg. When the murderer had come after Jimmy, knowing he was trapped in the wheelchair, Jimmy grabbed his flash camera. The popping blasts of light temporarily blinded the man, who stumbled, giving the police just enough time to get there.

"Inspired!" Put whispered. "Simply inspired."

28

Guts Lead To Glory

THE FOUR STARBUCK CHILDREN had broken just about every rule in the book, as far as normal family behavior was concerned. But it was hard to punish children who were being given medals for heroism and good citizenship from both the governor of Florida and the president of the United States.

They all had to get dressed up to go to the governor's mansion. Molly and Charly had worn their party dresses, but the patent-leather party shoes felt so stiff on their feet, which had been bare for so long, that they decided to wear thongs. Nobody was looking at their feet, however; from each of their ears a small chameleon dangled.

Living jewelry would have become the rage among youngsters if the Starbucks hadn't been fearful of animal abuse—especially in the north, where lizards could not stand the cold. So Madeline Starbuck had her designers at Starbuck Recital Wear whip up some rubber chameleon earrings. Like mood rings, they changed colors depending on the temperature. When held between the palms of your hands, they glowed a soft pink. In a cool breeze, they turned green.

A secretary had to be hired to handle the requests for television appearances and interviews. The twins and Robbie were in newspapers and magazines across the country. Their snapshots of Charly nearly getting eaten by the crocodile made it onto the front page of the *National Reporter* with the headline, "CROC SHOCK: Kids Save Baby Sis From Being Devoured." Another tabloid blared, "Tyke Versus Croc in Swamp Battle." There was a picture of Charly blasting through the surface, spurting water at the camera-stunned crocodile.

Things got so busy that Aunt Honey flew down to help the secretary. One day, shortly after Aunt Honey had arrived, they were all sitting at the table on the deck of the *Flagrant Flamingo*. Aunt Honey was wearing an immense hat that reminded Charly uncomfortably of her own brief moments on Cuda's head as a living hat. She was also wearing rhinestone sunglasses with swept-up frames that made her look like a jeweled bat.

"Now, children, I do feel that for the ceremony in the Rose Garden, when the president gives you and Robbie the National Citizenship Medal, it would be nice if you wore those uniforms I got for you, because I think they still have room at that military academy, and really it's so . . . so . . . ."

"So what, Honey?" Putnam Starbuck asked.

"Well, Put, you know, it looks so patriotic to be wearing a nice crisp uniform. I myself am planning to wear that wonderful white suit with the gold epaulettes. And who knows, they might have a twenty-one gun salute for our little heroes." She turned and pinched Charly's cheeks.

Why don't we just stuff you in a cannon, Honey Buns, and blast you out as part of the twenty-one gun salute.

Charly giggled when she heard Liberty flash this and rubbed her cheek where Aunt Honey had pinched it.

"They are patriotic, Honey—with or without uniforms. They just kept the waters of America from being poisoned."

"You know my old skating partner, Pink Stubbins, the one whose uncle runs the military academy? Well, Pink's sister was a very close friend of the first lady, so when we're in the Rose Garden at the White House, I thought I might mention this . . ."

Gads, she's going to make all those roses shrivel up and die.

"I think they're doing it again, Madeline." Honey spat out the words as Madeline walked from the galley with a platter of ham sandwiches.

"Doing what again, Honey?"

"That mental thing of theirs. It's so annoying. I know they're talking about me behind my back."

We're right in front of you, old Honey Guts. Molly smiled sweetly at her aunt.

Just then the phone rang. Charly jumped up to get it.

"Yes, yes," she was saying. "I'm not sure. Let me ask my dad. Daddy?"

"Yes, Charly?"

"Do we have an agent?"

"That's me for now. Who's on the phone?"

"Steven Spielberg."

29

Outside the Nick of Time

JUSTICE FOLLOWED SWIFTLY for the three toxic-waste criminals—Cuda, Sculp, and Ghee. Their New York connections were uncovered, and soon the entire ring of crooks had been revealed and were under indictment. Putnam was pleased with the swiftness of the court's action, and with the stiff fines and long prison terms. The children cheered the afternoon they heard that Cuda, Sculp, and Ghee were definitely out of business and in prison for the next fifteen years.

But for some creatures it was still too late. Although legal justice had been served, it had not been quite in the nick of time, and there were victims. One night just after dinner, not long after all the excitement, July was looking at a newspaper when he saw a small article buried at the bottom of page eight. The headline caught his eye. "Lavender Dolphin Washed Ashore North of Miami."

July raced up to the room he shared with Liberty.

It's Moon Spirit, isn't it? She seemed to sense something was wrong even before he showed her the article. He walked slowly to the hammock where Liberty swung and handed her the paper. She began to read.

"A strangely colored dolphin washed ashore on the beach of the Silver Grotto Hotel in the early morning hours yesterday. The dolphin, which people describe as having a lavender hue, was found by Melvin Finkelstein, a retired ear, nose, and throat doctor from South Orange, New Jersey. Dr. Finkelstein found the dolphin when he was walking on the beach near dawn.

" 'I was just walking along,' reported Dr. Finkelstein, 'and I saw this beautiful lavender thing shimmering in the early morning light. I had no idea it was a fish . . . fish don't come in those colors. I thought it was maybe a lady's nightgown.' "

A lady's nightgown! Liberty flashed. *How dare he!* She continued reading aloud.

" 'But it was beautiful, just beautiful. It had a magical quality to it, even in death,' Dr. Finkelstein said in an interview in his condo.

"Authorities will be taking the dolphin to the sea aquarium where veterinarians will perform an autopsy."

Liberty folded the paper and looked up at the colored skylight over her head. She sought out the piece of lavender glass and remembered the night, not so long ago, when the crescent moon had risen and appeared through the skylight like a dolphin leaping in the night sky.

We have to go back, she flashed. *We have to go back just one last time to see the others.*

I know. You're right, Liberty, you're right.

30

Moon Riders

MOONLIGHT struck the slide. There was a soft swoosh and then another. They slipped quietly into the water and swam to the *Little Coconut*. Charly, Molly, and Robbie were waiting. Liberty and July had agreed to take them. It was only fair. July poled them out of the cove into the more open water.

"Look, there's Bandit," Liberty whispered as she raised the sail. Overhead, the great bird spread its wings.

They headed down the silvery path that stretched out across the Gulf in the direction of Lonely Key.

"Do you think they'll like us? Do you think they'll like us? Which one will I get to ride? Is it hard to hang on?" The little twins' questions clamored in the night air.

"What if they don't come?"

Nobody even wanted to think of that possibility. But it was one. Liberty and July had not seen the dolphins since the night before they had gone into the mangrove swamp. They had accomplished their mission, but how would the dolphins know? They did not read newspapers, after all, and the twins, despite their medals of heroism, had been forbidden to ever go out again at night in the *Little Coconut* without an adult. But sometimes rules just had to be broken, and this was one of those times.

As they drew close to Lonely Key, they raised the daggerboard of the *Little Coconut* and coasted in on a wave. July and Liberty hopped out and dragged the boat high up on the beach. It had been so long since they had first come to the beach for the turtles. In another few months it would be time for the turtles to begin their egg laying once more. When that happened, July and Liberty had promised to bring Zanny, but not tonight. Tonight was for them, the children. No grown-ups allowed.

They waded into the surf. The little twins were between Liberty and July, and next to July was Robbie. They were all holding hands. The water lapped around them.

"Do you think they'll come?"

"How will they know we're here?"

"Oh, please, let them come."

Molly and Charly were on the brink of tears.

Robbie was calm, however. He would be disappointed if the dolphins didn't come, but it hardly mattered compared to what it felt like standing in the water with these kids, knowing that they really cared about him—that so many people cared about him. Ever since he had met the Starbuck kids, he had felt that he could, in a funny way, hold hands with the whole world, that he could squeeze a hand and it would squeeze back. He did this just now, and July's hand squeezed his in return. Yes, it would be nice if the dolphins came, but even if they didn't, he would still be more than satisfied.

"Will they come? Will they come?"

"Hush!" ordered Liberty, and she bent over in the water that lapped around her waist and Charly's chest. She put her arm around Charly's shoulders. "Look!"

"It's like Christmas tree tinsel," Molly exclaimed.

What's that clicking in my head? Charly flashed.

It's me, little one! Crest clicked.

Who said that?

I heard it, too, Molly flashed.

All the children's feet had left the sandy bottom. They were swimming and ducking in the surf.

Look at all these silvery spots of light. Why, it's just like the . . .

But July cut off her thought. *Don't say it, twerps!*

And even the little twins seemed to sense that this was not the time or place to think about the Barbie Beach Mansion.

Instead Molly flashed, *Am I dreaming?*

No.

The message clicked in both their heads.

We are not dreams. We are real.

A face with gentle eyes full of curiosity and intelligence turned to the twins.

We are here for you.

And suddenly it was as if they were wrapped in scarves of silken bubbles. Liberty and July were riding Streak and Spray. Crest and her cousin, Spinner, were carrying Molly and Charly. Robbie rode Spray's sister, Streamer. Foils of silvery bubbles flowed behind them.

Where are we going? July asked.

Cobb's Reef.

But Moon Spirit is gone, Liberty flashed.

We know, clicked Streak. *But it is never too late to celebrate the memory.*

And so they went. Like silver arcs the dolphins rose and fell in the night sea as they made their way across the Gulf with the children on their backs. To Cobb's Reef they went, where they would make their leaps into the sky in honor of Lunsyphrr, Moon Spirit, descendant of Styllsphrr. The other dolphins were already there and had begun their leaps.

Hang on tight! the dolphins clicked to the children.

They dove, and then at unimaginable speeds, they raced to the surface, where they burst through the water in a rain of silver and leapt for the moon.

Liberty felt the air in cold blasts on her cheeks. The stars seemed to be racing toward her. The moon loomed, immense and sparkling. She seemed to inhale its silvery light, and suddenly it was as if all the colors of the spectrum filled her head.

> *I am here, I am here!* a voice clicked in her head. *I am here in the silver of the moon's light. I am here in the bright shadow of the moon's day. I am here now and forever.*

Liberty looked around. Charly, Molly, July, and Robbie were all riding high toward the moon—their faces glistening, their hair streaked back, their eyes alive, as the shadows of the water carried them toward the light of the moon. And for this one brief instant, they all knew deep in their hearts that they lacked no color in the universe, but shimmered with every hue and shade. They had touched the soul of Moon Spirit and her ancient line of dolphins.

As they arched toward the moon, the five children felt the spirit of the white dolphin descend upon them. They became spectrums of light flying through the night. They felt the colors streaming through them like bright banners. They became living, breathing rainbows in the tropical night sky.

Just off Coral Key an old man steered his boat. A half hour before he had picked up four *barqueros*—a young man, his wife, and two nursing twin babies. The babies were fretful and whimpering. Their mother's milk had run thin from her own lack of water, and the babies, no matter how much they drank, still felt hungry.

Valtero knew this happened to newborns, so he always brought some milk in bottles with him. But these two weren't taking to the bottle. Still, all in all, the family was in good shape, so he did not need to rush on this beautiful starry night. The full moon had helped his old, dim eyes pick out the little family on the raft, but now he blinked and stared.

"*Santa Maria, Madre de Dios!*" he muttered. Then he blinked again. It was impossible. He had heard of the aurora borealis, the heavenly lights with their display of rainbow colors that drenched the northern night skies, but never had they spread their colors this far south. It must be a miracle. *Milagro!*

"*Mira, mira!*" he whispered to the man and his wife. They all looked up. High above in the sky, five smears of bright colors like rainbows streaked across the night and then dipped into the sea, sending up cascades of silver bubbles.

"*Milagro!*" the mother whispered. It was a miracle. Miraculous. "*Milagroso,*" she sighed, and the little baby twins stopped whimpering, looked up, and began to coo gently into the warm night air.